RESERVOIR FISHERIES

RESERVOIR FISHERIES

By
Dr. Shivaji Gyanba Jetithor
Assistant Professor
Department of Zoology/Fishery Science
Yeshwantrao Chavan Mahavidyalaya
Tuljapur-413601 (Maharashtra)

DPH
DISCOVERY PUBLISHING HOUSE
INDIA

Published by:

DISCOVERY PUBLISHING HOUSE
4383/4B, Ansari Road, Darya Ganj
New Delhi-110 002 (India)
Phone : +91-11-23279245; 23253475; 43596065
E-mail : discoverybooksindia@gmail.com
discoverypublishinghouse@gmail.com
namitwasan9@gmail.com
web : www.discoverypublishinggroup.com

First Edition: **2023**

ISBN: 978-81-959169-5-5

Reservoir Fisheries

Printed at:
Infinity Imaging Systems
Delhi

Preface

I take this opportunity to express my gratitude to Dr. Vishwas B. Sakhare, Professor and Research Guide, Post Graduate Department of Zoology, Yogeshwari Mahavidyalaya, Ambajogai for suggesting the problem, keen interest, encouragement and helpful guidance throughout the course of investigation.

I am very much thankful to Shri Madhukarraoji Chavan (President), Shri Narendraji Borgaonkar (Founder Secretary), Shri Ulhasdada Borgaonkar (Secretary), Shri Baburao Chavan, (Member) of Balaghat Education Society for their valuable support during the progress of my research work.

I am thankful to Shri Anand Pandagale, President of Mahatma Phule Shikshan Prasark Mandal for giving permission to conduct the research work.

I would like to extend my special gratitude to Dr. P.S. Prayag, Principal, Yogeshwari Mahavidyalaya, Ambajogai for providing library and laboratory facilities during study period. Thanks are due to all the staff members of Yogeshwari Mahavidyalaya, Ambajogai for help during the study period.

I am highly thankful to Dr. Anil Sitre, Principal and Shri J.S. Mohite, Ex-Principal of Yeshwantrao Chavan College, Tuljapur, Dr. D.R. Mane, Director, Higher Education (Maharashtra), Pune, Shri Sambhajirao Bhosale, President, Panchrang Pratisthan, Tuljapur and Shri Dilip (Bhau) Bhosale, for their encouragement.

I am very much thankful to Shri S.S. Talikote and all the members of Jay Ambika Matsya Vyvasik Sahakari Sanstha Limited' for their help, furnishing background information pertaining to Harni (Katgaon) reservoir which came very handy to complete the present study. Thanks are due to Shri H.R. Birajdar, Assistant Fisheries Development Officer, Osmanabad for providing necessary data and valuable suggestions.

I have the pleasure to thank my friends Dr. Amol Late and Mr. Shital Samte for their valuable support during the progress of research work.

I express deep sense of gratitude to my father Late Shri Gyanba Dattoba Jetithor for his constant help and encouragement.

I am also thankful to my wife Sow. Vidhya for bearing all the domestic problems. I wants to thank my brother Sushilkumar for his help in many ways.

–Dr. S.G. Jetithor

Contents

Introduction

Fish is an item of food that is so nutritious-rich in easily digestible protein, calcium, iron, omega-3 fatty acids and vitamin A, especially retinol, so essential for prevention of blindness and for the proper development and growth of a child as well as for nursing and lactating mothers. Yet, it receives such a low priority as a food item in the scheme of things and this is a paradox in itself. Besides providing nutritional security, fisheries sector employs over 14 million persons (25% of whom belong to the poor, backward and tribal community) and generates over Rs. 72, 00 crores worth of foreign exchange. Its contribution to the national GDP and to the agricultural GDP too is not insignificant, being 1.07% and 4.96% respectively. Though India is the third largest producer of fish and occupies the second position in aquaculture production in the world, the per capita availability of fish is a mere 9 kg .It needs to be raised to a level of at least 12 kg and the prospects for such a development are promising as there is no dearth of physical resources which, if properly utilized, could produce about 9 million metric tonnes of fish annually.

The inland fisheries resources of India are vast and comprise of river systems with ramifications of tributaries and distributaries network of canals crisscrossing the country, scores of natural lakes, a large number of man-made reservoirs, estuaries and lagoons. The major rivers and their tributaries, transverse through varied geoclimatic zones displaying high diversity in their biotic and abiotic characteristics throughout their 28,000 km linear drift. These rivers possess a mosaic of varying biotopes ranging from lotic to lentic habitats. All these resources offer immense scope and potential for developing the capture fisheries. India being a country of continental proportions, the reservoirs are spread over diverse geoclimatic regions. The fishery potential of reservoirs in India is under developed. The surface water area of existing reservoirs in India is estimated tobe more than 3 million hectares. A large number of artificial impoundments have been created in different river basins of our country since independence for irrigation, power generation, flood control, and other water resource development projects. The inland fish production in the country has registered a phenomenal increase during the last 6 decades. As against 0.2 million t produced in 1951; the present production of fish (1998) in the country is estimated at 2.2 million t in capture sector. The domestic demand of fish in the country is required to be more than 13 million t. A scientific understanding of all the water bodies supporting capture fisheries is imperative in order to maximize production, on a sustainable basis.

In India, there are 19,370 reservoirs spread over in 15 states, covering an area of 3.15 million ha. The area is expected to grow further to 6 million ha in due course of time of 25 years (Desai, 2008). Tamil Nadu has the highest reservoir area followed by Karnataka and Andhra Pradesh. A realistic evaluation of fish production from reservoirs in India is elusive. Compared to the impressive volume of data generated by individual research workers and various institutions on limno-chemical variables and biotic communities, the estimates on fish catch remain grossly inadequate. Reliable fish catch statistics and yield estimates remain as the weakest link in the database on Indian reservoirs.

It is generally known that, in the inland capture fisheries sector, while rivers, estuaries and wetlands contribute very little to inland catch, the bulk of capture fish production is from reservoirs only. The reservoirs, vast in extent, therefore, happen to be important resources with high potential of inland fish production, and of providing employment and income to several rural and urban population around. Since the reservoirs are constructed primarily for hydel and irrigation purposes, the fish production from them is treated as by-product importance. This relegation is one of the reasons of poor fish yield from reservoirs. So much so, the reservoir fish industry could not make any remarkable progress as yet. Because of the country's growing demand for irrigation and power, new reservoirs have been coming up and thus this potential is expected to grow further giving ample opportunities of culture based capture fishing practices, provided these water bodies are managed scientifically for development of fisheries at on optimally sustainable level.

The work of reservoir fisheries development in India was done much earlier in erstwhile Madras Fisheries Department after the formation of Mettur reservoir across river Cauvery. Thus the erstwhile Madras Fisheries Department was the front-runner of reservoir fisheries development in India now inherited by Tamil Nadu Fisheries Department.

Actually, the systematic reservoir fishery investigations were initiated by Central Inland Fisheries Research Institute (CIFRI), Barrackpore (West Bengal) in year 1963. The institute took up a detailed study of fisheries of Tungabhadra reservoir in Karnataka and Damodar Valley Corporation reservoirs (Konar, Panchet and Tilaiya) in Bihar. Later, an

All India Coordinated Research Project on Ecology and Fisheries of Freshwater reservoirs was launched by Indian Council of Agricultural Research through CIFRI. This project was eco-oriented so as to have in-depth study of all determinants of reservoir productivity of five reservoirs located one each in five states (Uttar Pradesh, Tamil Nadu, Andhra Pradesh, Bihar and Himachal Pradesh) in different eco-climatic conditions. Prior to inception of this co-ordinated research project, fisheries of four reservoirs of Damodar Valley Corporation (Bihar) and three in Madhya Pradesh were also studied. Subsequently, some more reservoirs of other states were also included in the investigation, for providing recommendations to manage them on scientific lines.

As per the mandate of CIFRI, each identified reservoir was studied at least for 2-3 years round the year by its scientists. In order to cover more number of reservoirs, the institute proposed a rapid survey of reservoirs with seasonal sampling, during pre-monsoon, monsoon and post-monsoon periods, in a year or two. The survey conducted by CIFRI for reservoirs in Karnataka, Andhra Pradesh, Maharashtra, Tamil Nadu and Madhya Pradesh states gave encouraging results in the sense that fish production potentiality of some of the reservoirs could be assessed to suggest measures for development of their fisheries. Accordingly, many of the reservoirs were found productive, facilitating the taking of necessary steps in this direction.

River water is usually running or flowing water. Construction of dam results in the creation of a reservoir or dam-lake, in which the lotic water of the upper reaches becomes lentic as water approaches the dam. Rise in reservoir depends upon river flow and rain water. A new reservoir passes through three trophic phases-initial fertility, trophic depression and final fertility. Filling of a reservoir inundates vast area bearing a cover of vegetation. It starts decaying and putrefaction results initial fertilization of the water leading to an intense development of fish food in the form of benthic micro and macro flora and fauna. The initial increase of biota is often spectacular. After the initial high fertility, trophic depression phase sets in. This is cause by gradual diminishing of the rate of nutrient release. This is due to increase in the volume of the impounded water and available nutrients used by the vegetation. After this phase is passed the final fertility level is reached in the reservoir, which is a much lower level than that of initial fertility.

A reservoir has its own peculiarities in which it differs from natural lakes. The riverine ecology of the water of the upper reaches becomes increasingly changed into lacustrine ecology in the reservoir. The benthic riverine fauna disappears and it is replaced by typical lacustrine benthic fauna. With the change in from the lotic to lentic conditions of the water current, riverine plankton are replaced by lacustrine plankton. The turbidity level also reduced as reservoir act as settling basins. Fish fauna is greatly affected. The running water fish species become fewer or completely eliminated. Slow water fish species are predominant. Floating plants may come up, particularly in tropics where they create deoxygenating conditions or cause other serious ecological problems.

The dam in some way interferes with the ecology of the upper reaches of the river. Migratory fishes are completely wiped out from the upper reaches. This often leads to disturbances in the ecosystem especially with advantage to the prey. The reservoir itself may affect the ecology of the lower reaches of the river. Periodical discharge of sediments from the reservoirs may cause mud and silting in the lower reaches with serious consequences on the fauna. Reservoir acts as fertility traps, reducing the amount of dissolved plant nutrients which would otherwise be freely arriving at the lower reaches.

The reservoirs are man-made ecosystems. Besides adding substantially to fish production, they offer employment opportunities particularly to the people around who last a means of living because of the formation of reservoirs. While aquaculture in small water bodies such as ponds is capital-intensive, development of fisheries in reservoirs, a culture based capture activity, is labour intensive. In other words, the reservoir is an ecosystem where fluviatile and lentic conditions coexist. In reservoir, the quality of impounded water varies from watershed to watershed, and even within the same watershed depending on the soil, climate and human activities. It also varies with shape of the reservoir basin, photoperiod, wind action and quality of water change. Owing to these, variables, evaluation of water quality and productivity of the reservoir have to be made separately for different sets of ecological families of reservoirs sharing similar ecoclimate.

Productivity of a reservoir is dependent on its biogenic capacity to transform solar energy into chemical energy. The energy fixed at primary producer level passes through trophic chain and a fraction of it ends up as fish flesh. Therefore, the structure of different food biotic communities (trophic dynamics) assumes great significance to reservoir fisheries management. Shortening food chain will lead to higher rate of fish production but in reservoir management there is little scope for changing community structure of plankton to increase primary productivity. However, improved fish production can be achieved by altering the species spectrum of fish, stocked through application of a well planned pattern of stocking.

According to Sreenivasan (2000) when fluviatile conditions are altered by dam construction, the native fauna, especially the aquatic organisms, are altered. Some species dwindle, some are endangered and some disappear. However a few less desirable species preponderate and biodiversity is greatly affected. After construction of dams in the upper reaches, some important indigenous species decrease or disappear. In India, the much prized Mahseers, Trouts, Barbus etc. are the ones endangered. Contrary to exaggerated claims that creation of reservoirs increases fish production in the large reservoirs there is drastic reduction in the fishery of the river system. Dams, channelization and pollution have changed many of the world's rivers where they once supported desirable fish in commercial quantities. Catches in them now stand reduced to a lower level. Large reservoirs will never be sources, which an increasing population can look upon as a reserve waiting to be tapped.

Exposed to the warm tropical climate, these water bodies in our country are extremely productive and they harbour an enviable spectrum of fish genetic resources. Optimum utilization of these resources can lead to a man-fold increase in inland fish production, earning the country a place among the top inland fish producing nations of the world. As a result of the construction of dams under various multipurpose river valley projects, a number of fresh water impoundments have come into existence. These impoundments are called reservoirs or dam-lakes which represent the complex environmental and biological systems. Within a reservoir there is a great diversity of interactive components ranging widely in morphometrical, operational and biological characteristics.

Reservoirs are generally classified as small (<1000 ha), medium (1000-5000 ha) and large (>5000 ha), especially in the records of the Government of India (Srivastava *et al;* 1985). Jhingran and Sugunan (1990) classified the reservoirs as large (>1000 ha), medium (500-1000 ha) and small (< 500). Small reservoirs are managed like ponds and constitute a 'put and take' fishery. However, the medium and large sized reservoirs constitute a capture fishery resource but have to be managed through enhancement programmes. The hidden fish production potential of reservoirs has not so far been realized. So much so the yield gap continues to be large, the average productivity being only 20 kg/ha/yr against a possible yield of over 200 kg/ha/yr in the case of small reservoirs, 100 kg/ha/yr in the case of medium and 50 kg/ ha/yr for large reservoirs (Tripathi, 2007). A large number of active fishermen can be directly absorbed in fishing and a much larger number including refugees and oustees indirectly in ancillary activities comprising handling packaging, transport and marketing. It is a resource that could be developed properly with the smallest investment giving the largest benefit in terms of production, employment, income and livelihood for the 'have-nots'.

The main problem in developing the fisheries of reservoirs has been stocking with inadequate numbers of advanced fingerlings, small size of fingerlings stocked, skewed proportion of species, release of fingerlings (truly speaking advanced fry) at a wrong place and at a wrong time. In addition, many of the small and big reservoirs have also been stocked with tilapia which is now a dominant species in several reservoirs with landings comprising small-sized fish. Our love for the exotics has found another niche and reservoirs are being stocked with silver carp, bighead carp, grass carp and common carp to the detriment of indigenous fauna. Regional preferences and biodiversity issues have not been borne in mind while developing the reservoir fisheries. It is time that fast growing local species with a consumer preference and high economic value are also stocked with efforts to produce their seed close to the reservoir concerned. Commercial fishing in all reservoirs must be regulated with a strict rider on fishing effort and mesh size.

Unfortunately, majority of reservoirs are not being scientifically managed for fisheries. Only a handful of them have so far been harnessed along scientific lines, while the others are either half-heartedly managed or not managed at all. As compared to several developed countries, the per hectare fish production in Indian reservoirs is very poor, being only about 20-25 kg per year as against 88 kg in the USSR (Jhingran, 1983), 100 kg in Sri Lanka and 64.5 kg in large reservoirs of Thailand (Bhukaswan, 1977). Dixitulu (1999) mentioned that in case of reservoir fisheries, however, the developmental process has been tardy; remaining by and large, at the level as at the time the British withdrew, with the exception of a few reservoirs. It is to the credit of the British that, at quite a few reservoirs, they set up farms and also undertake stocking of the reservoirs. The process no doubt continued after independence, with the production being conspicuous in a very few reservoirs, below average in some, and low to very low in others. One of the main factors responsible for low fish yield from Indian reservoirs is the unscientific management practices which stem from the inadequate knowledge of the ecology and production functions of this biotope. Apart from the urgent need to take up all old reservoirs for proper appraisal of their present status and for taking up rational management and conservation measures, it is highly imperative to take up fisheries development work in new reservoirs right from the initial stage itself. Lot of progress has been made in several developed countries in deep water fishing in reservoirs and management of their fisheries. The neglect of this vast potentially rich fishery resource is all the more applling, in view of inadequate fish production in the country even to meet the protein demands of our exploding populations, let alone the export demands.

The present low level of fish production in Indian reservoirs can be attributed to inadequate management in as much as many of them have potential for production, from a productivity point of view. In many of the reservoirs, the high rate of the primary and secondary productivity is not chancelled to fish production. Insufficient understanding of the reservoir ecosystem often comes in the way for adopting effective management measures.

Reservoir fishery is essentially a stocking-cum-culture system. There is no sound database in the reservoir fisheries. Except in some states like Tamil Nadu it is difficult to get data on even total production of a state. In southern region of country, in Tamil Nadu the total annual fish production potential for reservoirs is about 2,000 tonnes, which indicates per unit area production of 40 kg (Sanskarasubbaiyan and Menon 1984). However, Sreenivasan (1998) mentions 52,000 hectare of reservoir area. Sugunan (1995) estimated 52 small, 8 medium and 2 large reservoirs with 48.50, 13.74 and 12.66

kg/ha/yr fish yield respectively. According to Sundaramoorthy (2008) Tamil Nadu has 52 reservoirs, which includes 1 large, 34 medium and 17 small reservoirs. The total water spread area of reservoirs in state is 52,055 ha. The average annual production from large, medium and small reservoirs is 16.62, 65.23 and 71.34 kg/ha. CIFRI (1998) surveyed Amaravathy, Palar- pornthalar, Uppar, Pillor, Gunderipallam and Varattupallam reservoirs of Tamil Nadu and revealed that the fish yield in Varattupallam was highest and lowest in Amaravathy. Taking into consideration the area of reservoirs and stocking density, it was concluded that the fishery management in Palar- Poranthalar is best followed by Amaravathy and uppar, while it was poor in Pillar. The actual fish yields obtained from the reservoirs are less compared to the production potentials estimated through primary production studies. This gives scope for enhancement of fish production from these reservoirs through judicious stocking and exploitation. Kerala being essentially a marine fisheries state, inland fisheries till recently did not receive much attention. There are 29,660 ha of reservoirs with a fish yield less than 15 kg/ha; mostly Tilapia (Sreenivasan, 1998). According to Sugunan (1995), state is having 7 small and 2 medium reservoirs with fish production of 53.50 and 4.80 kg/ha respectively. Further Sugunan also mentions, there are total 30 reservoirs with water-spread area of 29,635 hectare. Karnataka, the important maritime state, the marine fisheries in state is more dominant than inland fisheries, where a major finance has been expended for the development of marine fisheries. State is having 60 reservoirs with an area of 2.20 Lakh hectares (Annual Report, Dept. of fisheries 1994-95). However, IIMA (1985) mentions presence of 28 reservoirs with total water spread area of 1,51,624 hectares, the average fish production from which is about 23-35 kg/ha/yr. Sugunan (1995) mentions the total area under reservoir in the state is 4,37,291 hectares comprising 4,679 reservoirs of different categories. Andhra Pradesh has 2.143 lakh hectares of reservoirs of all sizes

(Sreenivasan, 1998). According to Rao (2008) Andhra Pradesh has 102 reservoirs, which includes 7 large, 26 medium and 69 small reservoirs. Total water spread area of reservoirs in state is 2,34,000 ha. Biswas (1990) mentions the total reservoir area of state is 1.6 lakh ha; while according to Sugunan (1995), the state is having 37 small, 29 medium and 3 large reservoirs having 188, 22 and 16.80 kg/ha fish yield respectively. IIMA (1985) estimates the average reservoir fish production of 37.43 kg. CIFRI (1998) also conducted the survey of nine reservoirs of Andhra Pradesh and found that most of the reservoirs have the necessary infrastructure for raising the seed and exploitation of the fishery and recommended that the co-operative societies need to be activated and given the responsibility of management. There is an immense scope to introduce cage culture systems in most of the reservoirs. This will enhance the yield from reservoirs and also provide additional employment.

All the Northern states are purely inland states from fisheries point of view. The average annual fish production from large, medium and small reservoirs in Rajasthan is 40 kg/ha, 100 kg/ha and 1160 kg/ha respectively. According to Chaudhary (2008) the water spread area of large, medium and small reservoirs in state is 0.70.1.40 and 0.40 lakh hectares.In Uttar Pradesh all the reservoirs are multipurpose. According to Directorate of fisheries, Uttar Pradesh, the state is having 2.83 and 1.62-lakh hectares area under large and small reservoirs respectively. Sugunan (1995) estimates 31 small, 13 medium sized and one large reservoir in the state having fish yield of 14.60, 7.17 and 1.07 kg/ha/yr respectively. Punjab has less potential for reservoir fisheries. There are four dams. The naturally available fish species are the major carps, Common carps, *Tor putitora, Labeo dero, Labeo bata, Mystus seenghala, Synothorax* etc. (IIMA, 1985). Himachal Pradesh has two large reservoirs, namely Gobindsagar and Maharana Pratap Sagar. There are also three small ones i.e., Chamera I and II and Pandoh. The total water area of these reservoirs is 42,200 ha at F.R.L. Two more reservoirs Mallana and Koldam are likely to add to the reservoir tally of the state, increasing the total area to approximately 3000 ha. A specific fishing policy for the development and exploitation of fish from the reservoirs in the state is in operation since 1976.

West Bengal, Sikkim, Orissa and Bihar are the states of Eastern region of India. In Orissa the total reservoir area is 99,061 ha (IIMA, 1985). Sreenivasan (1998) estimated about 1, 19,403 ha large, 9,246 ha medium and 65047 ha small sized reservoirs. According to Sugunan (1995), the state is having a total of 1442 reservoirs with an area of 1,98,198 ha. West Bengal is an important maritime state on the east coast of India having only 7 reservoirs, out of which two are major ones (IIMA, 1985). According to Sugunan (1995), the state is having six reservoirs with combined water spread area of 15,732 hectares. Mukherjee and Praharaj (2009) reported 23,567.88 hectares of reservoir area in West Bengal. No correct data on fish yield, number of reservoirs and stocking is available as the pond culture practices are more dominant than the reservoir fisheries. In Bihar, total reservoir area is about 50,000 hectares. There are 350 fishermen's co-operative societies in the state with total membership of 27,142, which are under control of state co-operative department. The functioning of these societies are not satisfactory and are dominated by influential persons who exploit the members.

Northeastern states with 8206 ha of reservoirs (Sugunan, 1995) gave fairly good results, 31.5 kg/ha, despite the cooler climate. It is reported that fishery of 34,443 ha of lakes were developed in Assam, yielding 100-150 kg/ha (Anon, 1991).

Western region comprises states like Goa, Madhya Pradesh, Gujarat and Maharashtra. In Goa there are 3 medium and 2 small reservoirs. The total reservoir water spread area in state is 3,460 hectares (Vernekar, 2008). Madhya Pradesh is purely an inland fish producing state. According to Sugunan (1995), the total number of reservoirs in the state is 32 with water-spread area of 460384 hectares. IIMA (1985) reported the large and small reservoirs with a total water spread area of 2.5 lakh hectares. The fish production for the period of 1974-75 to 1979-80 from selected reservoirs was varied from 0.20 to 87 kg/ha/yr (IIMA, 1985). According to Sreenivasan (1998), state is having 1.17-lakh hectare of reservoirs yielding an average fish catch of 26.46 kg/ha. The Gujarat has about 0.14 million ha. area under reservoirs (IIMA, 1985). Maharashtra, one of the largest states in the country in population and geographical area having a number of rivers like the Godavari, the Bhima, the Krishna, the Narmada, the Tapti and other several rivers and their tributaries having a total of 1600 km of river length. Sugunan (1995) mentions the total reservoir area in the state is 2,73,750 ha. However, according to Sreenivasan (1998), Maharashtra is endowed with 1,79, 430 ha. of reservoir area and the state produced 7.83 kg/ha fish from its reservoirs. However, IIMA (1985) worked out 1, 05,202 ha reservoir area comprising 72 reservoirs. Rathod (1989) mentions the total area in the state is about 3.01 lakh. Pathak (1990) is of the view that, the area under reservoirs in the state of 20 ha and above estimated to about 2, 36,157 hectares. Fisheries and/or ecology of some reservoirs in Maharashtra have been documented by Desai (1980), IIMA (1985), Sugunan (1995), Sreenivasan (1991), Valsangkar (1993 and 1980), Sakhare (1999, 2001 and 2006), Joshi (2006), Shastri and Bhogaonkar (2006), Chavan *et al* (2006), Kadam *et al* (2006), Mali *et al* (2006), Mohite (2006), Chavan (2006), Niture and Chavan (2009), Lokhande *et al* (2009), Kumbhar *et al* (2009) and Sakhare and Jetithor (2009).

Reservoir management strategy takes into account the prevailing environmental varieties and it comprises both capture and culture fisheries norms. Indian reservoirs are spread over various geoclimatic regions and their drainages represent different types of catchment areas. Besides, the varying design and purpose of dams make the reservoirs different in their hydrographic and morphoedaphic characteristics. All these diversities frustrate the efforts to evolve a common management strategy that can be universally applied to Indian reservoirs. Researches conducted in selected reservoirs, selected as types, help us in arriving at common strategies for a group of reservoirs. Harni (Katgaon) reservoir is one such water body that could represent several of Indian reservoirs. Therefore, ecology based fisheries investigations were carried out in this reservoir from October 2007 to September 2009 and the package was evolved to manage its fisheries with a scientific basis.

Meterology, Morphometry and Hydrography of Harni (Katgaon) Reservoir

Harni (Katgaon) reservoir (Fig. 2.1) is situated near Katgaon village in Tuijapur tahsil of Osmanabad district and is connected by an approach road of the length of 6.5 km from Solapur-Hyderabad-National Highway No. 9. This approach road takes off near the Khanapur stage on the National Highway. The project is constructed across Harni river, a tributary of river Bori, having catchment area of 190.624 km^2 (73.60 sq. miles) at the project site. The head works of the project were started in June 1961 and completed in June 1964. This project envisages construction of an earthen dam and includes other works such as ogee spillway with its appurtenant works, head regulator on right flank and canals on left and right flanks taking off from the same head sluice.

No village was submerged under this reservoir. The villages such as Katgaon, Khanapur and Darshnal of Tuljapur and Tandulwadi and Musti of Solapur taluka receive benefit due to the irrigation facilities under this reservoir. The salient features of Harni (Katgaon) reservoir are depicted in Table 2.1.

Fig. 2.1

Table 2.1: The salient features of Harni (Katgaon) reservoir

1.	Name of River	Harni
2.	Location	Katgaon village
3.	Sub basin number	19
4.	Water Spread Area (ha)	239
5.	Year of Construction	1964
6.	Length of earthen dam	2,163.975 meters
7.	Length of ogee spillway	276.025 meters
8.	Maximum flood discharge	58,490 cusecs
9.	Maximum height of dam in river bed	17.080 meters
10.	Gross storage capacity(Mcum)	12.580
11.	Live storage capacity (Mcum)	11.170
12.	Carry Over capacity (Mcum)	1.410
13.	Catchment Area (km^2)	190.624
14.	Length of irrigation channel Left flank canal (km) Right flank canal (km)	 27.355 14.481
15.	Irrigation potential (ha)	1,660

The climate of reservoir area is primarily dry. The rainy season starts from mid-June and remains till end of September. With onset of the rainy season there is an appreciable drop in temperature. From October to November the climate is humid. From mid-November to January it is winter. From February to March the climate is dry and from April to June it is summer. May is the hottest month. The average rainfall of area is 730 mm. Though the area is thought to belong to assured rainfall zone the area has experienced moderate, severe and acute drought conditions for more than 30% of the last 90 years. Hence the entire area comes under the category of drought area.

The relative humidity during the afternoons being 20%. During the southeast monsoon season, the humidity is as high as 80% in the mornings and 60% in the afternoons.

Fisheries Management of Harni (Katgaon) Reservoir

INTRODUCTION

The growth of fisheries cooperative movement in India can be traced back to 1913 when the first fishermen's society was organized under the name 'Karla Machimar Cooperative Society' in Ratnagiri district of Maharashtra. Fisheries cooperatives are functioning both the marine and inland sectors of Maharashtra and are contributing towards the development of small scale fisheries of the state.

Cooperatives are autonomous associations of persons coming together voluntarily and democratically managed to meet their common economic, social and cultural needs and aspirations. Today, although it might seem that the approaches to the problem have changed over time, the resources for better functioning of the cooperatives appear more viable than ever. In different sectors, cooperatives have reflected their potentiality and strength in terms of mobilization of internal resources. The major objective of cooperatives is mutual help among a group of people, with common objectives and goals. This is more relevant in fishing sector which is a group activity.

A remarkable feature of Maharashtra fishermen is their very broad outlook and a high degree of cooperative spirit. This has paved the way of the overall development of the community through self generated resources (Braj Mohan and Srinath, 2004). Maharashtra fishermen have an enviable quality of cooperating with each other for the causes of fish production and post-harvest operations for common benefit and professional welfare and to provide security to each other in times of need (Raje and Singh, 1993). The successful fisheries cooperatives are not only engaged in marketing but are also involved in the supply of operational inputs and credit to fishermen.

The conditions prevailing in the fisheries sector are, by and large, comparable to those in the field of agriculture. The small people predominate. They are poor, illiterate and helpless. Their product is extremely perishabile. They need guidance and assistance at all stages of operation. This will be possible only if they are provided with an institutional structure which is adequately modern and responsive to their needs. A cooperative would be their own organization, most appropriate, and managed by them for themselves (Kamat,1990). A major cause of collapse of the cooperative movement in fisheries was the absence of effective management (Annamalai, 1996). At a time when the very concept of cooperatives as an instrument of development stands undermined, surprisingly it is gaining ground under private initiative.

In this background, the study of cooperative society engaged in fishing of Harni (Katgaon) reservoir was conducted.

MATERIALS AND METHODS

Fishes for the study were collected with the help of local fishermen beside purchasing them from local markets. Three sampling stations distributed randomly in three different regions have been selected for the study. They include station I, at lentic, II at intermediate and III at lotic sector of the reservoir. The fish were brought to the laboratory and preserved in 5% formaline solution after noting their original colours. The identification of the fishes was done with the help of standard keys (Day 1878, and Talwar and Jhingran, 1991).

A questionnaire method was adopted to collect data on socio-economic status of fishermen community, fish catch per day and monthly income earned by fisherman. So also, personal contact method was used to obtain necessary information from fishermen's cooperative society and district fisheries development office for a period of October 2007 to September 2009.

FISHERMEN'S CO-OPERATIVE SOCIETY

The fishing rights of the reservoir are given on lease to the co-operative society named 'The Jay Ambika Matsya Vyvsaik Sahakari Sanstha Limited'. The society was established on 22/03/1978 under Maharashtra Co-operative Act with registration number of OSM/RSR-552 Date-22/03/1978. The initial capital was Rs. 480/- only.

At the time of registration there were a total of 49 members. The number of member has increased by about 2 times during the last 23 years. In the year 1987-88, the total number of members were 49. In 2001-2002 it increased to 51, further and in subsequent years finally the total number of members become 57 till January 2010. The members of the co-operative society belong to different castes and religions. These are the nontraditional fishermen like muslim (Islam), dhangar (bandi) and lingayat.

Socio-economic Study

All 57 members are not full time fishermen. All of them are part time fishermen. The study area is socio-economically backward. It is observed that 62.07% of respondents were illiterate. General opinion of the communities is that education does not really help, expect, perhaps in getting a government job. The members of the community feel that there is need for an educational system that would import those enabling skills in their chosen profession and in areas such as management and accounting.

The socio-economic study was made in different villages at the periphery of the reservoir. A study has been made on the existing co-operative society depending on the reservoir and their constraints with a view to identifying the probable solution to augment the fish production from the reservoir in a sustainable manner. Most of the resources from which the society members earn their livelihood have been studied. The earnings of a livelihood by fishers in these areas is a grave challenge to be met.

The per capita annual income from fisheries range from Rs. 9000 to 37000/.50% of the fishermen reported an income in the range of 10,000 to 17,000 per annum. 27% fishermen get income from fisheries in the range of 18,000 to 22,000/-, and only 23% of the members get annual income in the range of 23000 to 37000/-. This range of variation in earnings indicates unreliability of fishing as a dependable occupation.

Agricultural labour and general labour are the two other occupations that these fishermen take for the purpose of gainful employment. Both these activities provide more working days and earnings than does the fisheries. It appears that fishing is only a minor activity compared to other economic actitivites. Women seem to have more working days in agriculture and other areas, than do men. From the point of view of the sources of income, fisheries in Harni (Katgaon) reservoir provide only 24% of the family income. General and agriculture labour provide 76% of the family income. It should be noted that most people, both men and women, shift from one type of job to another based on season. Both agriculture and fisheries provide work during the season. When the season is over, people shift to general labour, wherever available.

All the respondents were members of the co-operative society and the study shows that they were also active in the banking transactions. Marriage, house construction, acquisition of milch animals, cycles and fishing equipments constitute the major purposes for which bank loans are availed. It can also be seen from this study that 8.75 of the respondents possessed *Pucca* house and some of them possessed bicycle, black and white television. Radio, cow and land. The study revealed that only 60% fishermen have their own nets. 62.5% inhabitants do not have ownership rights on a agricultural land through which they can earn a living. The socio-economic status of fishermen is presented in Table 3.1.

Table 3.1: Socio-economic status of fishermen

Name or resource	% of occurrence
1. Agriculture and land owners	37.5
2. Pucca houses	8.75
3. Sanitory	18
4. Electricity	69.5
5. Mobile users	2
6. Cycle users	72
7. Motor cycle users	2
8. Cow (more than 2 numbers)	38
9. Fishing nets	60
10. Radio	32
11. Black and white television	10

From the above socio-economic analysis, it can be seen that the fishermen are rightly termed as the poorest among the inhabitants around the reservoir.

Lease Amount

The fishing activities in Harni (Katgaon) reservoir were undertaken immediately after its formation in year 1964. According to the lease policy introduced by the Maharashtra government; the fisheries department leases the fishing rights of the Harni (Katgaon) reservoir to the co-operative society for fishing on contract basis every year. During 2007-08, the lease amount was Rs. 24000/- on which the society was allowed to exploit fish from the Harni (Katgaon) reservoir. During 2008-09, the lease was Rs. 24800/-.

Seed Stocking

The society generally purchased fish seed from the Chandni fish hatchery, which is a government hatchery constructed near Paranda (in Osmanabad district), about 70 kms from the reservoir site. Details of fish seed stocked in the reservoir and stocking rate/ha for two years is shown in Table 3.2.

Table 3.2: Details of fish seed stocking in Harni (Katgaon) reservoir

Year	Catla	Rohu	Mrigal	Silver carp	Grass carp	Common carp	Total	Stocking/ ha
2007-08	200,000	100,000	100,000	75000	100,000	100,000	6,75,000	2824
2008-09	60,000	40,000	30,000	–	10,000	20,000	1,60,000	669

During year 2007-08, the society purchased 6,75,000 fish seed, which gave a per hectare stocking density of 2824 fingerlings. In second year (2008-09) society could purchase 1, 60,000 seed, which gave per he stocking density of 669 fingerlings. But recently during year 2009-10 the reservoir was not stocked with seed. Usually the seed was purchased in the form of fry, and it was grown up to the fingerling stage in ponds constructed in the vicinity of reservoir. The fingerling stage is then stocked in reservoir.

Seed of major carps (*Catla catla, Labeo rohita, Cirrhinus mrigala*) and *Hypophthalmichthys molitrix, Ctenopharyngodon idella* and *Cyprinus carpio* were stocked in the reservoir. Silver carp was not stocked in year 2008-09. It was due to the non-availability of seed. Among the varieties, catla seed was stocked in large numbers when compared to the seed of others. The details of seed stocking are depicted in Table 3.2 and Fig. 3.1 and Fig. 3.2. The stocking rate/ha ranged from 669 (year 2008-09) to 2824 (year 2007-08), with an average of 1747 fingerlings/ha/yr.

Auto stocking was observed in Harni (Katgaon) reservoir. Carps have been observed to breed due to the availability of certain congenital factors. These factors vary from season to season depending upon the on-set of monsoon, quantum of rainfall, volume of water entering the reservoir etc. In reservoir Common carp (*Cyprinus carpio*) breed three times in a single year.

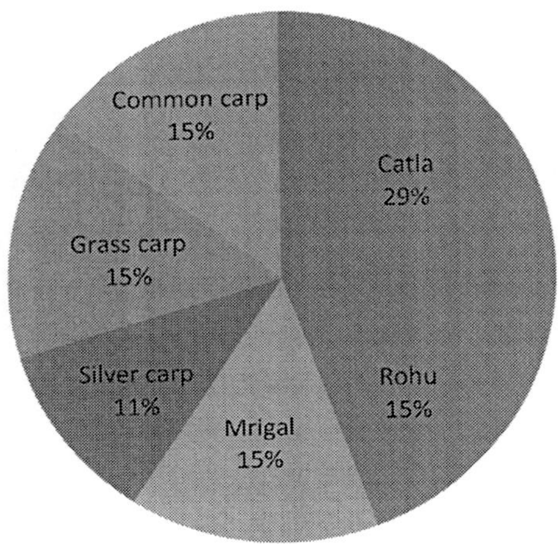

Fig.3.1:Seed composition during year 2007-08

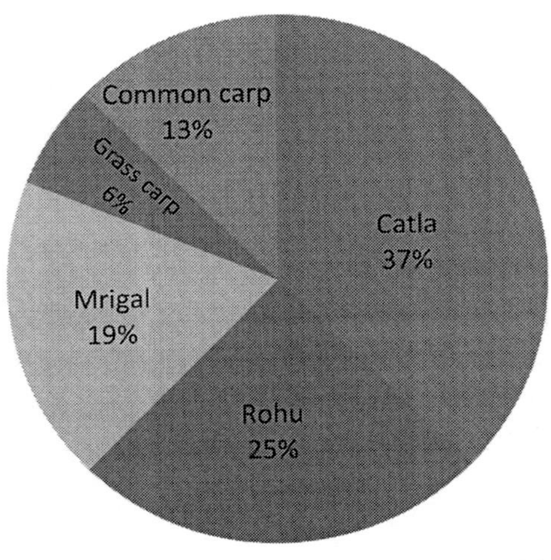

Fig.3.2: Seed composition during year 2008-09

Fish Fauna

A total of 37 fish species belonging to 13 families have been recorded from the reservoir (Table 3.3).Family cyprinidae contributed the largest number of species (17), followed by family bagridae and channidae (3 each). Family notopteridae, siluridae, mastaembelidae and ambassidae represented by two species each, while family cobitidae, claridae, heteropneustidae, mugilidae, anabantidae and gobiidae were represented by one species each.

Table 3.3: Ichthyofauna of Harni (Katgaon) reservoir in Osmanabad district

Class: Pisces **Subclass: Teleostomi** **Order: Clupeiformes** **Suborder: Notopteroidei** **Family: Notopteridae** 1. *Notopterus notopterus (Pallas)* 2. *Notopterus chitala (Ham.)*
Order: Cypriniformes **Suborder: Cyprinoidei** **Family: Cyprinidae** 3. *Chela phulo (Ham.)* 4. *Catla catla (Ham.)* 5. *Labeo rohita (Ham.)* 6. *Labeo boggut (Sykes)* 7. *Labeo fimbriatus (Bloch)* 8. *Cirrhinus mrigala (Ham.)* 9. *Cyprinus carpio (Linn)* 10. *Hypopthalmichthys molitrix (Sykes)* 11. *Ctenopharyngodon idella (Ham.)* 12. *Amblypharyngodon mola (Ham.)* 13. *Discognathus modestus (Ham.)* 14. *Osteobrama cotio (Ham.)* 15. *Puntius sarana sarana (Ham.)* 16. *Puntius ticto ticto (Ham.)* 17. *Puntius chola (Ham.)* 18. *Puntius sophore (Ham.)* 19. *Rasbora daniconius (Ham.)*

(Table Contd...)

Family: Cobitidae 20. *Nemacheilus botia (Ham.)*
Order: Siluriformes **Family: Bagridae** 21. *Mystus cavasius (Ham.)* 22. *Mystus seenghala (Sykes)* 23. *Mystus vittatus (Bloch)*
Family: Claridae 24. *Clarias batrachus (Linn.)*
Family: Heterpneustidae 25. *Heteropnesutes fossilis (Bloch)*
Family: Siluridae 26. *Wallago attu (Bloch and Schneider)* 27. *Ompak bimaculatus (Bloch)*
Order: Mugiliformes **Family: Mugilidae** 28. *Mugil cephalus (Linn.)*
Order: Channiformes **Family: Channidae** 29. *Channa gachua (Haml.)* 30. *Channa striatus (Bloch)* 31. *Channa marulius (Ham.)*
Order: Mastacembeliformes 32. *Mastacembelus pancalus (Ham.)* 33. *Mastacembelus armatus (Lacepede)*
Order: Perciformes **Family: Anabantidae** 34. *Anabas testudineus (Bloch)*
Family: gobiidae 35. *Glassogobius giuris (Ham.)*
Family: Ambassidae 36. *Chanda ranga (Ham.)* 37. *Chanda nama (Ham.)*

Fish Catch

The fishery is exploited by fishermen who have been organized from village Katgaon into a co-operative society. The details of fish catch from the reservoir for the period of 2007-08 to 2008-09 is shown in Table 3.4. The maximum fish catch was recorded during year 2007-08. It gave an average fish production of 83.68 kg/ha/yr. The minimum production was during 2008-09 at 9600 kg, giving an average fish production of 40.16 kg/ha/yr. During the study period the catch of carps showed the higher catches than those of local fishes (Table 3.4).

Table 3.4: Total fish catch and per hectare fish prduction

Year	Local fishes (kg)	Carps	Total catch	Fish production/ha
2007-08	5000	15,000	20,000	83.68
2008-09	2400	7,200	9600	40.16

The stocked landings dominated over the unstocked species. Important fishery comprised fishes such as *Catla catla, Labeo rohita, Cirrhinus mrigala, Hypophthalmichthys molitrix, Cyprinus carpio,* and *Channa spp.* A rare appearance of silver carp in the landings indicates that fish is not suitable in Harni (Katgaon) reservoir.

Fishing days and closed Season

In Harni (Katgaon) reservoir fishing is carried out throughout the year. No closed season has been declared by the district fisheries department. However, on the suggestions of district fisheries department, the society has framed some rules for the conservation of fish. For example, catching of fish belonging to Indian major carps less than 1 kg has been prohibited. Such types of fish if caught, it should be immediately released in the reservoir. This rule is not followed by fishermen members.

Overexploitation and Improper Fishing System

The over exploitation of the reservoir plays a major role in extinction of the species. The co-operative society deliberately issues the license to any number of fishermen. Many fishermen from Solapur district migrate to this area during rainy season and catch huge quantity of fish. This has adversely affected the livelihood of permanent local fishermen. Over exploitation of the reservoir for fishery has resulted in excessive mortality and reduction in effective population size of the fish. Monsoon is the breeding season for most of the fishes and the fishing activity is at peak during this season.

Conservation of Breeding Grounds

There is an urgent need to breed some important fish species in reservoir for maintaining the stock of fish species. Side by side the breeding grounds should be restored scientifically. Otherwise, the productivity will not sustain for a longtime; and after a period ranging from one to several years, the fish yield will definitely decline to an alarming level. Several autobreeding grounds had been found to be lost because of indiscriminate fish catching by fishermen, loss of eggs, spawns etc of different fish species due to the use of mosquito net by fishermen of the reservoir. District Fisheries Department has taken various steps for building up awareness among the fishermen against the use of mosquito nets conservation of brooders etc through publicity and awareness camps. Besdies, several training programmes were also organized by fisheries department for capacity building among the fishers depending on the reservoir.

Restriction to Net Usage

In Harni (Katgaon) reservoir fishing is carried out throughout the year. No closed season has been declared by the district fisheries department or the co-operative society. Fishing activity is at its peak during the monsoon season. A majority of the total fish catch is during the monsoon season. Since monsoon is the breeding season for most of the fishes, it is advisable to ban fishing of native fishes. This can be achieved by restricting the net sizes being used by the fishermen. Only large sized gill nets should be allowed during monsoon, which are useful to catch introduced fishes. Even after the monsoon season, the present restriction on minimum net size should be strictly followed so as to catch only mature fishes.

Permanently Stopping Migrating Fishermen

Fishing licenses should be issued to permanent fishermen residing near the reservoir and moderate reservoir who are solely dependent on the reservoir for their livelihood. The present status of fisheries in the reservoir and moderate reservoir productivity indicates the depletion of fish resource. In order to reduce the fishing pressure, it is advisable to avoid migratory fishermen from fishing. Since their fishing period is monsoon, large quantities of brooders are destroyed by overfishing.

Fishing Gears and Crafts

The major fishing gear in reservoir is surface gillnet. The net is made of nylon twine. Presently, the plastic twine (mono-filament) nets are also being used in the reservoir. Dragnets are also used especially for catching catfishes and weed fishes. The other fishing gears such as cast nets, long lines and traps are also operated but the catches are insignificant. The presence of underwater obstacles restricts the use of active gear in reservoir and the choice is often limited to passive gear such as gillnets.

The thermocoel platform of 6×3.5 feet size is used as fishing craft. It is covered by a plastic covering. This craft is not suitable to carry large nets which are heavy.

The wooden boats are operated only during monsoon season. These boats are taken on lease from fishermen of nearby reservoir.

Coracle, a saucer shaped country craft, is also used in Harni (Katgaon) reservoir. It is made of a split bamboo frame, covered with buffalo skin. Apart from being simple and inexpensive, coracle is durable. It is also a versatile craft used for laying and lifting of nets, besides navigation and transport of fish and other material. The members of cooperative society purchase the craft individually without any financial assistance from co-operative society or fisheries department.

DISCUSSION

Devi (1997) reported the socioeconomic status of fishermen engaged in fishing of two reservoirs in Hyderabad city. The survey indicated the percentage of literacy at 74%. The survey also showed that almost all the respondents owned houses, either pucca or semi pucca house or kaccha houses.

During present investigation it is observed that 8.75 of the respondents possessed Pucca house and some of them possessed bicycle, black and white television. Radio, cow and land. The study revealed that only 60% fishermen have their own nets. 62.5% inhabitants do not have ownership rights on a agricultural land through which they can earn a living.

Mohan (2002) reported economic status of fishermen of Malampuzha reservoir in Kerala. 79.17% of respondents were literate, though the literacy is largely confined to primary level (45.83%). Both agriculture and fisheries provide work during the season and most of people, both men and women, shift from one type of job to another based on season.

The per capita annual income from fisheries of Harni (Katgaon) reservoir range from Rs. 9000 to 37000/.50% of the fishermen reported an income in the range of 10,000 to 17,000 per annum. 27% fishermen get income from fisheries in the range of 18,000 to 22,000/-, and only 23% of the members get annual income in the range of 23000 to 37000/-. This range of variation in earnings indicates unreliability of fishing as a dependable occupation.

Agricultural labour and general labour are the two other occupations that these fishermen take for the purpose of gainful employment. Both these activities provide more working days and earnings than does the fisheries. It appears that fishing is only a minor activity compared to other economic actitivites. From the point of view of the sources of income, fisheries in Harni (Katgaon) reservoir provide only 24% of the family income. General and agriculture labour provide 76% of the family income. It should be noted that most people, both men and women, shift from one type of job to another based on season. Both agriculture and fisheries provide work during the season. When the season is over, people shift to general labour, wherever available. Thus, it can be well concluded that the fishermen engaged in fishing of Harni (Katgaon) reservoir are poor.

The enhancement of fisheries through stocking of fish seed has been a common practice throughout the world. It has emerged as one of the most widespread management tools for inland fisheries, for the reason that it has often been biologically successful. Many of the states are practicing stocking activities in their own rivers, lakes and reservoirs in order to enhance production and for the purpose of stock improvement. The reason for this shift in approach is that the more conventional approaches to management by control of fishing have proved incapable of limiting fishing efforts, and for compensating the short fall of recruitment caused by overfishing and environmental damage. Many stocking programmes are carried out in India without properly defined objectives or evaluation of the potentials or actual success of the exercise, despite considerable evidence of improvements in the yield from fisheries all over the world, achieved through application of measures for revival of fisheries based on defined objectives.

In any stocking activity, planning and a stepwise approach for the implementation of the plan is the most important aspect to be considered so as to take care of the ecological and practical aspects and to ensure that the activity is a successful one. Guidelines are available in many countries in respect of stocking exercises, which are often species specific or related to a particular type of water body. It is an essential part of stocking strategy to identify its objectives, and mechanisms by which it will be carried out, keeping in view the potential ecological and environmental risks. Appropriate implementation strategies are inevitable for ensuring the success of the stocking programme.

Stocking density is an important factor that determines the success or failure of the whole programme and hence this needs to be assessed carefully. To determine the optimum stocking density, factors such as ecological characteristics, and existing biomass should also be considered (Lalrinsanga *et al.* 2006).

There exists a very high complexity of factors for deciding on the most appropriate size or age of the fish to be stocked. The reason is that these are known to vary from species to species and place to place. Paucity of information in this regard is one of the main factors, leading to the complexity referred to. The optimal size for stocking is mainly chosed by considering two factors; viz; cost and survival. Stocking of fish at very small sizes leads to risks associated with high mortality even though the cost of stocking material increases exponentially with length. This mortality –size relationship also provides the basis for a quantitative assessment of stocking density. However, other factors such as biology and life history traits of the species are also vital tools to be considered.

Stocking policy is specific to a reservoir and decided by its biogenic capacity, the growth rate of stocked species, natural mortality, and losses to escape and predator pressure. Fish should be stocked in environments suitable for their sustenance and growth. They should grow quickly by being highly efficient in utilizing natural food. Fish species that feed low on the food chain are preferred, but they should also offer good eating, economic value and potential for marketing, either locally or in remote markets. Attempts to stock fry have done little to enhance production in Indian reservoirs. Studies suggest that fish fingerlings 70-100 millimeters (mm) and longer achieve better survival rates and good growth. Small reservoirs measuring less than 1,000 ha can be stocked at a rate of 800-1,000 fingerlings/ha, taking into account the impact of existing catfish in the ecosystem and also the likely loss by escape (Vass *et al.* 2009).

Normally a combination of different Indian major carps can be used to enhance the reservoir catch. The combination is determined by the vacant food niches identified previously. If the density of phytoplankton and zooplankton is high, equal proportions of *Catla catla* and *Labeo rohita* can be stocked. The percentage of *Cirrihinus mrigala* and *Cyprinus carpio* should be decided based on the benthic population and detrital load in the reservoir, but they should not be more than 30% of fish population, as they are difficult to harvest. If the system has a lot of *Hydrilla* and *Potamogeton,* grass carp can account for about 10% of stock to control vegetation while boosting fishery productivity.

Stocking species in appropriate ratios can help shift the composition in favour of economically valuable species over low-value ones.

Enhancing production through stocking should not endanger the sustainability and conservation of indigenous species, especially if ecologically sensitive species are present. Small reservoirs should not be converted into production systems. Stocked species should not exceed 60-70% of the fish population, with indigenous species accounting for the remainder. The number of seed required is estimated on the basis of the proposed stocking density, targeted production amount, area of the water body, species combination, fingerling availability and cost including transportation to reservoir site, and budget.

Raghavacharis and Surychandra Rao (1984) and recommended the following stocking rates:

1. Large reservoirs (above 5000 ha) - 200 fingerings/ha
2. Medium reservoirs (1000-5000 ha) - 400 fingerlings/ha
3. Small reservoirs (less than 1000 ha) - 1000 fingerlings/ha.

In the present study the reservoir came under small category. During 2007-99 the stocking rate was more and it was less during 1999-2000 when compared with recommendations of Raghavacharis and surychandra Rao (1984).

The fish fauna is an important aspect of fishery potential of a water body. Fish fauna of Indian reservoirs has been studied by several workers. It is observed that the distribution of fish species is quite variable because of geographical and geological conditions (Sakhare and Joshi, 2003).

Srinivas (2007) reported ichthyofauna of Edulabad reservoir (Andhra Pardesh) representing 13 species of cypriniofrmes, 9 species of siluriformes, 4 species each of channiformes and perciformes. The fish fauna consisted a major carps, minor carps, catfishes, murrels, tilapias, and other food fishes. Of these rohu, catla, grass carp and tilapias were found to be most abundant.

Vinod *et al.* (2007) recorded 29 fish species from Umiam reservoir of Meghalaya. Of the 29 species, 21 were native fish species, 5 were introduced native species and two species were the exotic fish species introduced in reservoir.

Mahapatra (2003) reported 43 species of fishes from Hirakud reservoir of Orissa, out of 43 species, about 18 were of economic importance. According to him *Labeo rohita* has a dominant presence among Indian major carps and *Mystus aor* is dominant among the catfishes.

Chandanshive *et al.* (2007) recorded fifty-nine species of fishes in Pavana river of Pune. Wagh and Ghate (2003) studied fish fauna of the rivers Mula and Mutha.

Shinde *et al.* (2009) recorded 15 fish species belonging to 3 orders, 4 families and 12 genera from Harsool dam of Aurangabad district, Maharashtra. The order cypriniformes found dominant with 11 species, followed by perciformes 3 species and siluriformes with 1 species.

Hiware (2006) studied ichthyofauna from four districts of Marathwada region of Maharashtra and recorded sixty-six fish species belonging to 16 families. The ichthyofauna consisted of carps, catfishes and trash fishes.

Ahirrao and Mane (2000) studied icththoyfauna from Parbhani district of Maharashtra.

Sakhare (2001) recorded 23 fish species belonging to 7 orders in Jawalgaon reservoir of Solapur district in Maharashtra.

Sakhare and Joshi (2003) reported 34 fish species from reservoirs of Parbhani district in Maharashtra.

Charak and Fayaz (2006) studied the ecological status of Salal reservoir in Jammu and Kashmir. They reported only 10 species of fishes. The paucity of fish fauna in the reservoir may be due to the mountain barrier separating the area from rest of the state.

Fish biodiversity and fisheries potential of Udai sagar reservoir of Udaipur (Rajasthan) was studied by Rathore *et al* (2017). The reservoir supports fish fauna of 31 species representing 9 families, where Indian major carps dominated the catch by contributing 90 per cent to the total landings.

The fish community of the Haro reservoir of Rajasthan in relation to physico-chemical parameters was studied by Sisodiya *et al* (2018). They reported 15 fish species belonging to 5 families.

Sharma *et al* (2020) studied ichthyofaunal diversity and reported 27 species of fishes belonging to 7 orders from Dilawara reservoir where order cypriniformes was dominant.

Pathak and Mudgal (2005) identified 29 species of fishes in Virla reservoir with order cypriniformes contributing maximum of 19 members (65.51%) of species followed by 4 members (13.70%) of order ophiocephaliformes.

Ravinder *et al* (2016) reported 14 species of fishes from Dharmasagar reservoir of Warangal district, Telangana state.

Ichthyofaunal diversity of two reservoirs (Chandrasagar and Ramanpad) of Mahabubnagar district of Telangana was reported by Reddy and Parameshwar (2015). A total of 19 fish species belonging to 3 orders were recorded in Chandrasagar and 32 species belonging 6 orders were recorded from Ramanpad reservoir.

Information on fisheries management status of Pechiparai reservoir in Tamil Nadu was documented by Chrispin *et al* (2016). Increased fish seed stocking and fish effort through share fishing system increased the total catch of reservoir from 3.5 kg/ha/yr (1962-80) to 13 kg/ha/yr (1981-2015). This increase in fish production was due to considerable contribution by stocked vareties especially Indian major carps.

Nagma and Khan (2015) reported occurrence of 31 fish species belonging to 5 orders, 11 families and 21 genera from Pili reservoir of Bijnor district of Uttar Pradesh.

Sakhare (2009) reported 21 fish species belonging to 10 families from Ramdara reservoir in Osmanabad district of Maharashtra. Sakhare (2007) studied ecology and fisheries of Wan reservoir in Beed district of Maharashtra. He accounted 25 fish species from Wan reservoir. These include carps, catfishes, featherbacks, and other. Sakhare (2002) confirmed the occurrence of 28 fish species in Palas-Nilegaon reservoir of Osmanabad district of Maharashtra. In the present investigation on Harni (Katgaon) reservoir it was noted that species occurrence was very much similar to that recorded earlier by Sakhare (2002, 2007, 2009) and Ahirrao and Mane (2000). The observed similarity could be due to the presence of these reservoirs in same geographical and climatic region of Maharashtra.

In a study on similar lines Sakhare and Joshi (2003) recorded 28 fish species from Palas-Nilegaon reservoir in Osmanabad district. This includes 9 species of carps, 5 of catfishes, 2 of featherbacks, 5 of livefishes and 7 belonging to miscellaneous fishes.

Mahapatra (2003) accounted 4.34 kg.ha/yr fish yield from Hirakud reservoir of Orissa.

Vinod *et al.* (2003 b, 2007) estimated the per hectare fish yield for Umiam reservoir (Meghalaya) in the range of 65.52 to 97.87 kg/ha/yr.

Kumar and Verma (2002) studied ecological status of Masanjore reservoir of Jharkhand. The average annual fish yield was recorded at 12.8 kg/ha. The population of *Labeo calbasu, Cirrhinus mrigala,* and *Cyprinus carpio* constituted more than 90 per cent of the commercial catches. The predatory fishes were represented by *Wallago attu, Mystus seenghala,* and *Channa spp.* These predators prey on the fry and fingerling of carps resulting a decline in major carp fish landing and reduction in the population of *Labeo rohita* and *Catla catla.*

Namboothiri (2008) reported increase in fish yield of Malampuzha reservoir (Kerala) from 6.2 kg/ha (in 1990-91) to 24.05 kg/ha (in 2006-07).

Srinivas (2007) mentioned average fish production from Edulabad reservoir in Andhra Pradesh at 208.83 kg/ha/yr, which was still much higher than Indian average reservoir fish production of 29.7 kg/ha/yr. The fish production from Edulabad reservoir is much higher when compared with the data obtained during the present study.

In Harni (Katgaon) reservoir the fish production is poor as a whole, the growth of the fish shows that there is scope for obtaining optimum yield. Considering the overall ecology of the Harni (Katgaon) reservoir it is important to note that there is possibility for a better yield of fish if managed scientifically. Physico-chemical and biological factors exhibited the productive nature of Harni (Katgaon) reservoir.

The closed season for fishing is to allow the brood fishes to migrate uninterrupted for spawning and thereby increase the natural recruitment in the reservoir. In Gandhi Sagar reservoir, the closed season is strictly observed (Dubey, 2008). In Harni (Katgaon) reservoir fishing is carried out throughout the year. No closed season has been declared. Similar practice is observed in Jaismand reservoir (Jhingran, 1985) and in several reservoirs of Bihar and Haryana (Srivastava *et al.* 1985).

Baiju and Hridayanathan (2002) reported gill-nets, cast nets, lines, traps, drag nets as main fishing gears in Muvattupuzha river system of Kerala.

In Hirakud reservoir of Orissa gill nets and long line are commonly used (Mahapatra, 2003). Operation of shore seines (drag nets) is banned in the reservoir, as these have small meshes and are indiscriminately operated. Very few fishermen use cast net and rod line for fishing. Hooks and line (long line) are mostly used to catch cat fishes and Indian major carps. Some fishermen use tubes of wheels of motor cars while operating small gill nets.

In Gandhi Sagar reservoir of Madhya Pradesh gill nets with floats, drag nets, and long lines are used (Dubey, 2008).

Namboothiri (2008) accounted multifilamentous nylon gill nets, cast nets, trammel nets, simple wooden traps and hook and line from Malampuzha reservoir of Kerala.

The available information confirms that in all Indian reservoirs gill nets are the common gears (Sakhare 2007, Mahapatra 2003, Dubey 2008, Namboothiri, 2008).

Baiju and Hridayanathan (2002) accounted dugout canoes and plank built canoes from Muvattupuzha river system of Kerala.

Dubey (2008) reported plank built flat bottom boats, Bengal type of dingies and mechanized boats from Gandhi Sagar reservoir.

Crafts used for fishing in Malampuzha reservoir mainly constitute inflated tubes (Namboothiri, 2008).

Sakhare (2001, 2007) described primitive type of crafts from reservoir of Maharashtra. Crafts are nothing but a platform of 6×3 feet size with a depth of 4-10 inches. This is prepared from thermocoel and covered by a plastic covering. Similar type of craft is also used in Harni (Katgaon) reservoir.

Physico-chemical Environment

INTRODUCTION

Aquatic ecosystem is the most diverse ecosystem in the world. The first life originated in the water and first organisms were also aquatic where water was the principal external as well as internal medium for organisms. Thus water is the most vital factor for the existence of all living organisms. Water covers about 71% of the earth of which more than 95% exists in gigantic oceans. A very less amount of water is contained in the rivers (0.00015%) and lakes (0.01%), which comprise the most valuable fresh water resources. Global aquatic ecosystems fall under two broad classes defined by salinity – freshwater ecosystem and the saltwater ecosystem.

Freshwater ecosystems are inland waters that have low concentrations of salts (< 500 mg/l). The salt-water ecosystem has high concentration of salt content (averaging about 3.5%). An aquatic ecosystem (habitats and organisms) includes rivers and streams, ponds and lakes, oceans and bays, and swamps and marshes, and their associated animals. These species have evolved and adapted to watery habitats over millions of years. Aquatic habitats provide the food, water, shelter, and space essential for the survival of aquatic animals and plants. Aquatic biodiversity is the rich and harbours variety of plants and animals from primary producers algae to tertiary consumers large fishes, intermittently occupied by zooplankton, small fishes, aquatic insects and amphibians. Many of these animals and plants species live in water; some like fish spend all their lives underwater, whereas others, like toads and frogs, may use surface waters only during the breeding season or as juveniles. The study of freshwater habitats is known as limnology. Freshwater habitats can be further divided into two groups as lentic and lotic ecosystems based on the difference in the water residence time and the flow velocity. The water residence time in a lentic ecosystem on an average is 10 years and that of lotic ecosystem is 2 weeks. In lotic ecosystem, the average flow velocity ranges from 0.1 to 1 m/s whereas lentic ecosystems are characterized by an average flow velocity of 0.001 to 0.01 m/s (Wetzel, 2001; UNEP, 1996). The lentic habitats further differentiate from lotic habitats by having a thermal stratification with is created in a lake due to differences in densities. Water reaches a maximum density at 4° C, a warm, lighter water floats on top of the heavier cooler water thus creating thermally stratified zones which corresponds to epilimnion, the warm layer, the hypolimnion, the colder layer separated by a barrier called thermocline. The lotic ecosystem is characterized by stream orders depending on the origin and flow and various types of stream pattern namely dendritic, radial, rectangular, centripetal, pinnate, trellis, parallel, distributary and annular, which determines the flooding and soil erosion hazards of the region. However, the basic unity among these ecosystems is that any alteration in the catchment area of these ecosystems will affect the water quality of both lotic and lentic ecosystem. The catchment area is all land and water area, which contributes runoff to a common point, which may be a lake or a stream. The term catchment is equivalent to drainage basin and watershed

(Davie, 2002; Tideman, 2000). The term lotic (from lavo, meaning 'to wash') represents running water, where the entire body of water moves in a definite direction. It includes spring, stream, or river viewed as an ecological unit of the biotic community and the physico-chemical environment. Lotic ecosystems are characterized by the interaction between flowing water with a longitudinal gradation in temperature, organic and inorganic materials, energy, and the organisms within a stream corridor. These interactions occur over space and time.

Water quality, habitat structure, flow regime, energy source and biotic interactions are the major environmental factors that determine water resource integrity (Karr, 1991). The physical and chemical attributes of water are the critical components of a water resource. They include temperature, dissolved oxygen, pH, hardness, turbidity, concentration of soluble and insoluble organic and inorganic, alkalinity, nutrients, heavy metals, and an array of toxic substances which may have simple chemical properties or their dynamics may be complex and changing, depending upon other constituents in the geological strata, soils, and land use in the region (EPA,1990). The human effects on biological processes can result in mortality or may shift balance among species as a result of subtle effects, such as reduced reproductive rates or changing competitive ability.

Both fresh and salt water also form the habitats for innumerable organisms, such as seaweed, shellfish, crabs and other marine life that are components of human nutrition. In Europe and North America, impaired health and reproductive disorders were observed in aquatic animals and animal species that derive their sustenance from the water (Ellenberg, 1988). The causes were discovered to be contaminants in the water, such as organochlorines, e.g., DDT and other insecticides, and organic heavy metal compounds, e.g. methylmercury, which had been assimilated by the animals via their skin and respiratory systems or through food chains with associated concentration (biomagnification). Methylmercury compounds are considerably more toxic than elementary mercury and its inorganic salts. Human exposure to methylmercury comes exclusively from consumption of fish and fish products and prenatal life is more susceptible to brain damage than adults (Fitzgerald. and Clarkson, 1991). Nonetheless, these discoveries represented only the beginning; a large number of other contaminants were subsequently diagnosed and their dispersal paths identified.

In addition to restrictions in the utilization of water bodies as sources of drinking water, or other uses, contamination of fresh water and marine water can also have a multitude of indirect deleterious effects on human beings such as disruption of community and traditional activity, economic and nutritional hardships. It is therefore of overriding importance to find and improve means of monitoring and evaluating water quality and pollution levels in order to remedy and/or prevent harm to human beings and their environment.

Reservoirs are human-engineered habitats that occur in almost all major river basins in the world. Because these systems are a prominent feature of the landscape and are of high economic and recreational value, it is important for aquatic ecologists to understand how they function.

At present there are about 40,000 reservoirs with the total stirage capacity approximating 6000 km^3 on the earth; this amount is nearly equal to the global water consumption volume planned for the beginning of the 21st century (Zilov,1999).

The majority of limnologists refer reservoirs to a subtype of lakes differing only in the way of information. However, reservoirs radically differ from lakes both in absolute (age, place in a catchment area, configuration, location of a maximum depth area, origin of bottom sediments, direction of chemical gradients, location of water discharge area, etc.) and in relative indices (water surface area vs. water catchment area, water exchange time, water level fluctuations, hydrodynamic features etc).Evidently, these differences dictate the necessity of using not only common but quite different approaches to water quality control in lakes and reservoirs.

The increasing industrialization, urbanization and developmental activities, to cope up the population explosion have brought inevitable water crisis. The health of reservoirs and their biological diversity are directly related to health of almost every component of the ecosystem (Ramesh *et al.*, 2007). In freshwater bodies, nutrients play a major role as their excesses lead to eutrophication. Excessive macrophytic vegetation is indicative of the eutrophication status of any water body. Monitoring of water quality is the first step that can lead to management and conservation of aquatic ecosystems. It is also true that the management of any aquatic ecosystem is aimed to the conservation of its habitat by suitably maintaining the physico-chemical quality of water within acceptable levels. Hence, in the present study, an attempt has been made to study the physico-chemical parameters of Harni (Katgaon) reservoir to arrive at certain conclusions on the structural and functional aspects of the reservoir and to suggest ways and means for its conservation.

MATERIALS AND METHODS

Monthly samples were collected from the three stations for a period of two years from October 2007 to September 2009. The water samples (at a depth of one meter) were collected with the help of sampler in the morning hours. Water samples were brought in one-liter plastic containers to the laboratory for analysis. Parameters like temperature, transparency, pH, dissolved oxygen, free carbon dioxide, and alkalinity were analyzed at the study sites, whereas parameters viz. the total dissolved solids, total hardness, and chlorinity were analyzed in the laboratory.

The methods used for the analysis of various physicochemical parameters are as given in methodology for water analysis (Kodarkar *et al;* 1998, Trivedy and Goel, 1984 and APHA, 1985).

Phyisco-chemical Analysis:

1. Temperature (°C)

The atmospheric temperature and surface water temperature were recorded with a centigrade thermometer having 0.1° C division and a range of 00 to 50° C.

2. Hydrogen Ion Concentration

The hydrogen ion concentration (pH) values were recorded at the water sample collection sites with the help of Hanna made pH meter.

3. Transparency (cms)

Transparency of water was measured by a Secchi disc of 20 cm diameter with four quadrants by on upper surface painted alternate black and white, tied with a marked nylon rope for measurement. The secchi disc was lowered into the water with the help of a graduated rope to a hook in the center. Two readings of depth; one at a point when the disc just disappears (A) and the other at which it reappears (B) was taken as Secchi disc transparency in cm.

$$\text{Secchi disc transparency (cm)} = \frac{A + B}{2}$$

4. Total Dissolved Solids (mg/l)

The total dissolved solids were determined with the help of digital TDS Meter No: EQ: 670 (Equip-Tronics). The result were expressed as mg/1

5. Dissolved oxygen (mg/l)

The water samples were collected in glass stoppered oxygen bottles. One ml of manganese chloride and one ml of alkaline potassium iodide was added with help of pipette. It was thoroughly mixed and then brown precipitate was allowed to settle. Then in to each sample few drops of concentrated Hcl was added drop wise through the side of bottle and was well shaked to dissolve the precipitate 100 ml of the above solution was taken in conical flask, and few drops of 1% starch indicator was added which turns the solution to blue color. This solution was titrated against N/80 sodium thiosulphate till the colour disappears.

1 ml of N/80 $Na_2S_2O3.5\ H_2O$).1 mg of O_2

1 ml of N/80 $Na_2s_2O_3$. 5

Total hardness (mg/l) ($CaCO_3$)=H_2O= 0.0001 gm of O_2

Volume of O_2 in water= V×70/U ml of O_2/Liter at NTP

Where V= Volume of sodium thiosulphate used for titration

U= Volume of sample water taken.

6. Phenolphthalein Alkalinity (mg/l)

100 ml of sample taken in a conical flask and 2 drops of phenolphthalein indicator added. If it remained colourless that showed phenolphthalein alkalinity as absent. If it was turned pink. It was titrated with 0.1 N Hcl to a colourless end point.

$$\text{Phenolphthalein Alkalinity } Caco_3 \text{ mg/l} = \frac{(A \times \text{Normality}) \text{ of Hcl} \times 1000 \times 50}{\text{ml of sample}}$$

Where A = ml of Hcl used with phenolphthalein

7. Total Alkalinity (mg/l)

2-3 drops of methyl orange indicator were added to the solution in phenolphthalein alkalinity was already determined. This was titrated with 0.1N Hcl to the end point, when the colour changed from yellow to pink.

$$\text{Total Alkalinity as } CaCO_3 \text{ mg/l} = \frac{(B \times \text{Normality}) \text{ of Hcl} \times 1000 \times 50}{\text{ml of sample}}$$

Where, B= ml of total Hcl used with phenolphthalein and methyl orange

8. Free carbon dioxide (mg/l)

Free CO_2 was analyzed at sites by using phenolphthalein indicator and sodium hydroxide 100 ml of sample was taken in conical flask and few drops of phenolphthalein indicator were added. If the color turns pink, free CO_2 is absent. If it remained colourless, it was titrated against 0.05 N NaOH till the pink colour appears.

$$\text{Free } CO_2, \text{ mg/l} = \frac{(\text{ml} \times \text{N}) \text{ of NaOH} \times 1000 \times 44}{\text{ml of sample}}$$

9. Chlorides (mg/l)

10 ml of sample was taken and few drops of k_2CrO_4 added. The sample was titrared against 0.02 $Agno_3$ to obtain yellow to brick red end point.

$$\text{Chlorides (mg/l)} = \frac{V \times N \times 35.45 \times 1000}{v}$$

Where V = Volume of titrant in ml

N = 0.02 (normality of $Agno_3$)

v = Volume of sample in ml.

10. Total hardness (mg/l)

50 ml of water sample was taken and 1 ml of ammonia buffer and a pinch of NaCN (inhibitor) was added. Then a pinch of Erichrome Black T indicator was added. The sample was titrated against 0.01 m EDTA solution until a end point of wine red to blue colour appeared.

$$\text{Total hardness (mg/l) } (CaCO_3) = \frac{T \times 1000}{V}$$

Where, T = Titrant in ml.

V= Sample in ml.

RESULTS

Temperature (°C)

Seasonal variation in air and water temperature are presented in Table 4.1, 4.2, 4.3 and 4.4.

During 2007-2008, in the summer the mean air temperature values recorded were 36.05, 37.05 and 37.2° C at stations I, II and III respectively. While its minimum value in summer was 32.2° C at station II in May 2007, maximum was 41° C at station III in April 2008. The corresponding mean values in 2008-2009 were 36.3, 37.3 and 34.75° C at stations I, II and III respectively. Its minimum (35° C) was recorded at station II & III in February and maximum value (40° C) was noticed at station I in April 2009.

Table 4.1: Monthly values of Air temperature (°C) (Year 2007-2008)

Stn.	Oct.	Nov.	Dec.	Jan.	Feb.	Mar.	Apr.	May	June	July	Aug.	Sept.
I	27	27	30	31	34	39	37	35.4	32	34	29	30.2
II	23	27.4	28	33	37	40.2	40	32.2	33.2	30	30.5	33.3
III	25.5	32	30	31.5	35	36	41	36.8	30	33	34	29.8

Table 4.2: Monthly values of Air temperature (°C) (Year 2008-2009)

Stn.	Oct.	Nov.	Dec.	Jan.	Feb.	Mar.	Apr.	May	June	July	Aug.	Sept.
I	26.2	27	25	29.4	29	36.9	40	39.4	35.6	34.2	29.4	29.2
II	25	27.8	29.2	30	35	38.8	39	35.5	33.8	29.9	30.2	29.4
III	27	29.2	26.4	30.2	36	37.5	39.4	38.8	32	30.8	28.7	28.6

Table 4.3: Monthly values of Water temperature (°C) (Year 2007-2008)

Stn.	Oct.	Nov.	Dec.	Jan.	Feb.	Mar.	Apr.	May	June	July	Aug.	Sept.
I	17	18.2	19	20	31	29	30	32	28	23	23	26
II	17	18.1	20.2	21	30.8	29	32	31	29	22	24	25
III	18	20	18	20	31	31.8	32	32	29.5	24	23	26

Table 4.4: Monthly values of Water temperature (°C) (Year 2008-2009)

Stn.	Oct.	Nov.	Dec.	Jan.	Feb.	Mar.	Apr.	May	June	July	Aug.	Sept.
I	17	17	18	19.5	30	29	30	31.8	32	23	24	25
II	17.5	18	19	18	29.1	29	31	32	30	24	24.5	25.6
III	18	17.5	19	18	29.8	28	32	31	31	23	24	26

In monsoon the average air temperature values were 31.3, 31.5 and 31.7° C at stations I, II and III respectively. During this period its minimum (30° C) was noticed in June at station III. The corresponding average values in 2008-2009 were 31.3, 31.5 and 31.7° C at stations I, II and II respectively. While its minimum (28.6° C) was seen in the September at station III, maximum (35.6° C) was recorded at station II in June.

In winter the average air temperature was 27.5, 27.8 and 29.7° C in II, III sampling stations and I respectively. While its minimum (23° C) was recorded at station II in October, maximum (33° C) was found at station II. Its corresponding values during 2008-2009 were 27.5, 27.8 and 29.4° C at stations I, II and III respectively. Its maximum value recorded was 30.2° C in January at station III, while minimum value was 25° C at station II in October 2008.

During the study period water temperature ranged between 29° C- 32° C in 2007-2008 in summer, minimum temperature (29° C) was recorded in March at II and maximum temperature (32° C) at I in May. The corresponding values in 2008-2009 was noticed in the range of 28-32° C. Its minimum value (28° C) was recorded in March at station III, while its maximum (32° C) was recorded at station III & II in April and May.

In monsoon the water temperature ranged between 22 to 35° C. The mean water temperature values were 25° C, 25° C and 25.6° C at stations I, II and III respectively. While its minimum (22° C) was found at station II in July, maximum value (29.5° C) was recorded at station III in June 2008. The corresponding mean values recorded during the monsoon 2008-2009 were 26, 26.2 and 26° C at stations I, II and III respectively. During this period temperature ranged between 23° C to 32° C. Its maximum value (32° C) was recorded in June at station I, June, while minimum value (23° C) at station I&III in August.

During 2007-2008 winter the mean water temperature recorded was 18.55, 19.7 and 19° C in stations I, II and III respectively. The water temperature ranged between 17° C to 21° C. While minimum (17° C) was noticed in October at station I & II, maximum temperature (21° C) was found at station II in January. During the second year (2008-2009), the mean water temperature found was 17.8, 18.1 and 18.1° C at stations I, II and III respectively. While its minimum (17° C) was found at I in October and November, maximum value (19° C) was recorded in month of December at station II and III.

pH (Potentia Hydrogeni)

Seasonal variations in pH at different spots in Harni (Katgaon) reservoir are presented in Table 4.5 and 4.6.

Table 4.5: Monthly values of pH (Year 2007-2008)

Stn.	Oct.	Nov.	Dec.	Jan.	Feb.	Mar.	Apr.	May	June	July	Aug.	Sept.
I	8.0	8.1	7.7	7.5	8.1	8.4	8.0	8.0	6.8	7.1	7.4	7.2
II	7.6	7.9	7.4	7.3	8.4	8.4	8.0	8.2	7.3	6.9	7.5	7.2
III	7.7	7.3	8.1	7.2	8.2	7.9	8.4	8.3	6.5	7.0	6.9	7.1

Table 4.6: Monthly values of pH (Year 2008-2009)

Stn.	Oct.	Nov.	Dec.	Jan.	Feb.	Mar.	Apr.	May	June	July	Aug.	Sept.
I	8.0	8.4	7.5	7.6	8.2	8.5	8.0	8.1	6.9	7.0	7.3	7.1
II	7.8	7.7	7.2	7.5	8.3	8.1	7.9	8.2	7.1	6.8	7.2	6.9
III	7.6	7.2	7.3	8.0	7.9	8.4	8.1	8.0	7.1	7.5	7.1	7.0

In first year summer 2008, the mean pH values of 8.1, 8.2 and 8.2 were recorded at stations I, II and III respectively. The corresponding mean summer values in second year were 8.2, 8.1 and 8.1. During first year of investigation, the minimum pH of 8 was recorded at station I in April and 7.9 was at station II in April 2009, while the maximum recorded was 8.4 at station II in February 2008 and 8.4 at station I & II in March and 8.4 at station III in April 2009.

In monsoon 2008, the mean pH values of 7.1, 7.1. and 6.8 were recorded at stations I, II and III respectively. In monsoon 2009 they were 7.0, 7.0 and 7.1 at I, II and III respectively. During this season a maximum pH of 7.5 was found at stations II in August 2008. While the minimum pH of 6.5 was recorded at station II in June 2008 and 6.9 at station I in June 2009.

In winter the mean pH values at three spots was 7.8, 7.5 and 7.5 in 2007-08 and corresponding values in 2008-2009 were 7.8, 7.5, and 7.5. During this period the maximum of 8.4 at station I in 2008, while a maximum value of 8.1 was recorded at station I and station III in in November and December 2007.

Transparency (cms)

The transparency values at three sampling stations of the Harni (Katgaon) reservoir for the period of two years are presented in Table 4.7 and 4.8.

Table 4.7: Monthly values of Transparency (cms) (Year 2007-2008)

Stn.	Oct.	Nov.	Dec.	Jan.	Feb.	Mar.	Apr.	May	June	July	Aug.	Sept.
I	82	83	89	90	90	115	115	125	64	50	53	50
II	82	84	85	100	92	117	117	127	66	49	52	51
III	80	75	88	100	91	118	118	127	65	59	53	39

Table 4.8: Monthly values of transparency (cms) (Year 2008-09)

Stn.	Oct.	Nov.	Dec.	Jan.	Feb.	Mar.	Apr.	May	June	July	Aug.	Sept.
I	82	85	90	97	91	97	114	122	66	50	54	52
II	83	84	88	98	92	98	116	124	69	48	52	50
III	82	84	85	100	92	96	118	123	67	49	53	51

The mean transparency values during summer 2008 were 106.2, 108.5 and 108.5 in stations I, II and III respectively. While its minimum value (90) was noticed at station I in February, maximum value (127) was recorded in May at station II & III. The corresponding mean values in 2009 were 106, 107.5 and 107.2 at stations I, II and III respectively, while its minimum (91) was recorded at station I in February and maximum (124) was noticed at station II in May 2009.

In monsoon of year 2008, the mean transparency values recorded at I, II and III were 54.25, 54.55 and 54. In 2009 the corresponding values were 55.5, 54.7 and 55. In year 2008, minimum value (39) was recorded at station III in September and its maximum (66) was found at station II in June. During the year 2009 the minimum value (48) was noticed at station II in July, while maximum value (69) was noticed at station II in June.

During year 2008 winter season, the mean transparency values at three stations of study were 87.25, 87.75 and 88.5, while in second year, the corresponding values were 88.5, 88.2 and 87.7 at stations I , II and III respectively. During first year winter the maximum (100) was recorded at station II and III in January 2008. During second year winter, the minimum of 82 was recorded at station I and II in October and maximum of 100 in January 2009 at station III was recorded.

Total Dissolved Solids (mg/l)

The values of total dissolved solids (TDS) expressed in mg/l for the two years period are presented in Table 4.9 and 4.10.

Table 4.9: Monthly values of Total Dissolved Solids (mg/l) (Year 2007-2008)

Stn.	Oct.	Nov.	Dec.	Jan.	Feb.	Mar.	Apr.	May	June	July	Aug.	Sept.
I	105	116	115	128	195	280	198	185	98	103	106	108
II	100	115	120	121	180	296	190	190	95	105	112	89
III	98	118	122	120	192	280	196	188	110	198	96	90

Table 4.10: Monthly values of Total Dissolved Solids (mg/l) (Year 2008-09)

Stn.	Oct.	Nov.	Dec.	Jan.	Feb.	Mar.	Apr.	May	June	July	Aug.	Sept.
I	110	122	130	128	190	260	198	220	103	117	111	103
II	115	120	123	130	180	292	198	200	104	118	114	99.7
III	114	119	127	130	199	198	222	235	106	110	116	102

During year 2008, the mean seasonal value at the three stations were 214.5, 214 and 214 in summer, 103.7, 100.2 and 103.5 in monsoon and 114.5, 114 and 114.5 in winter. The corresponding values during 2009 were 217, 217.5 and 213 in summer, 108.5, 108.9 and 108.5 in monsoon, and 122.5, 122 and 122.5 in winter.

The seasonal minimum values in the first year summer were 180 at station II in February and in monsoon it was 90 at station III in September and in winter it was 98 at station III in October. In the second year of the investigation, a minimum of 180 at station II in February (summer), 102 at station III in September (monsoon) and 114 at station III in October (winter) were recorded.

The seasonal maximum values in the first year of studies were 296 at station II in March (summer), 198 at station III in July (monsoon), 128 at I in January (winter). In the second year the maximum values of 292 at station II in March (summer), 118 at station II in July (monsoon) and 130 at station II & III in January (winter) were recorded.

The observation on TDS for two years (2007-2008 and 2008-2009) clearly indicate that the TDS values were high in summers followed by winter and monsoon.

Dissolved Oxygen (mg/l)

Dissolved oxygen contents of water samples from three stations along the Harni (Katgaon) reservoir are computed in Table 4.11 and 4.12.

Table 4.11: Monthly values of Dissolved oxygen (mg/l) (Year 2007-08)

Stn.	Oct.	Nov.	Dec.	Jan.	Feb.	Mar.	Apr.	May	June	July	Aug.	Sept.
I	9.1	8.8	8.1	5.8	4.3	4.8	4.5	4.4	8.3	9.1	9.3	9.8
II	9.2	8.3	8.3	6.0	4.4	4.9	4.3	4.6	8.4	9.4	9.6	9.8
III	9.1	8.2	8.1	6.3	4.2	4.7	4.1	4.7	8.5	9.3	9.4	9.7

Table 4.12: Monthly values of Dissolved oxygen (mg/l) (Year 2008-09)

Stn.	Oct.	Nov.	Dec.	Jan.	Feb.	Mar.	Apr.	May	June	July	Aug.	Sept.
I	9.7	8.7	8.4	6.9	6.1	5.7	4.9	4.4	8.2	9.2	9.5	9.8
II	9.3	8.4	8.3	6.8	6.2	4.8	4.6	4.2	8.5	9.3	9.4	9.7
III	9.4	8.6	8.6	6.4	6.3	5.1	4.2	4.3	8.3	9.2	9.3	9.6

During the first year (2007-2008) of the study the dissolved oxygen ranged between 4.1 to 9.8 mg/l and seasonal dissolved oxygen values at the three stations (I, II and III) were 4.5, 4.5 and 4.4 (summer), 9.1, 9.3 and 9.2 (monsoon) and 7.9, 7.9 and 7.9 (winter) respectively. In summer the minimum value (4.1) was observed at station III in April and maximum of (4.9) was found at station II in March.In winter minimum (6) was found at station II in January, while maximum (9.2) was found at station II in October.

During the second year (2008-2009) of the study, the dissolved oxygen ranged from 4.2 to 9.8. In summer the seasonal mean values of 5.2, 4.9 and 4.9 were found at stations I, II and III respectively, while its minimum (4.2) was found at station II in May. In monsoon the mean values were found to be 9.1, 9.2 and 9.1 at three sampling stations. The minimum (8.2) value was found at station I in June, while maximum value (9.8) was found at station I in September. In winter the mean dissolved oxygen values were 8.4, 8.2 and 8.4 at stations I, II and III respectively. While its minimum (6.4) was recorded at station III in January, maximum (9.7) was recorded at station I in October.

Phenolphthalein alkalinity (mg/l)

Monthly values of phenolphthalein alkalinity are presented in Table 4.13 and 4.14.

Table 4.13: Monthly values of Phenolphthalein Alkalinity (mg/l) (Year 2007-08)

Stn.	Oct.	Nov.	Dec.	Jan.	Feb.	Mar.	Apr.	May	June	July	Aug.	Sept.
I	30.9	31.1	31.2	31.8	25.4	27	27.5	27.4	27.9	28	29.2	30
II	30.4	30.9	30.9	31.4	25.2	27.4	27.8	27.9	28	28.4	29.5	30.4
III	30.8	30.4	31	30	26	27.8	27.1	27.6	28.1	28.6	29.9	30.6

Table 4.14: Monthly values of Phenolphthalein Alkalinity (mg/l) (Year 2008-09)

Stn.	Oct.	Nov.	Dec.	Jan.	Feb.	Mar.	Apr.	May	June	July	Aug.	Sept.
I	30.8	28.7	31.6	31	23	24	25.6	26.8	27.9	28.1	29	30
II	31.8	31.4	31.4	23.5	23.5	24.8	25.9	28.4	27.6	28.6	29.4	30.1
III	31.6	31.2	31	30	23.2	24.9	25.2	27	28	28.9	29.5	30.2

The seasonal mean values of phenolphthalein alkalinity during 2007-2008 summer were 26.8, 27 and 27.1 mg/l at station I, II and III respectively. Its minimum (25.2) was found at station II in February, while its maximum (27.9) was found at station II in May. The corresponding mean values in summer of second year (2008-2009) were 24.8, 25.6 and 25 at station I, II and III respectively. While its minimum value (23) was noticed in February at station I in February 2009.

During monsoon (2007-2008), the mean values in three stations were 28.7, 29 and 29.3. While its minimum (27.9) was found at station I in June, its maximum (30.6) was recorded in September at station III. The corresponding mean values in 2008-2009 was 28.75, 28.9 and 29.1 at station I, II and III. The minimum (27.6) was found in June at station II, while its maximum (30.2) was recorded at III in September.

During winter (2007-2008) the mean values were 31.2, 30.9 and 30.5 at station I, II and III respectively. While its minimum (30) was found at III in January, and maximum (31.8) was noticed at I in January. The corresponding mean values in the second year (2008-2009) of the present study were 30.5, 29.5 and 30.9 mg/l at station I, II and III. While its minimum value (23.5) was noticed during January at station II and maximum value (31.8) in October at station I.

Total alkalinity (mg/l)

Monthly values of total alkalinity are presented in Table 4.15 and 4.16.

Table 4.15: Monthly values of Total Alkalinity (mg/l) (Year 2007-08)

Stn.	Oct.	Nov.	Dec.	Jan.	Feb.	Mar.	Apr.	May	June	July	Aug.	Sept.
I	261	272.1	277	278	246	220	204	189	116	132	140	182
II	265	172.2	278	276	248.2	215	203	197	112	128	142	187
III	264	276.2	276	277	245	223	199	189	118	130	148	185

Table 4.16: Monthly values of Total Alkalinity (mg/l) (Year 2008-09)

Stn.	Oct.	Nov.	Dec.	Jan.	Feb.	Mar.	Apr.	May	June	July	Aug.	Sept.
I	261	265.1	270	275.1	251	225	209	194	116	130	140	188
II	260.1	267.5	271.8	276.3	252.2	220	208	192	117	123	148	189
III	266.2	265.2	273	271.4	250	228	204	194	119	129	146	185

During the year 2007-2008, the station-wise mean values of the total alkalinity in summer were 214.7, 215.8 and 214 mg/l at station I, II and III respectively. Its minimum (189) at III in May and maximum (248.2) were found at station III in February. In monsoon, the mean values were 142.5, 142.2 and 144.2 mg/l. The minimum (112) was observed in June at station II and maximum (187) was found at station II in September. In winter the mean values were 272.02, 272.8 and 273.3, minimum (261) at station I in October and maximum (278) were found at station II & I in December and January respectively.

During the year 2008-2009, the mean values of total alkalinity were 219.7, 219.05 and 219 in summer, 143,144.2 and 144.7 in monsoon, and 267.8, 268.6 and 268.9 in winter at station I, II and III respectively. In summer, the minimum value (192) was noticed at station II in May, while the maximum value (252.2) was found at station II in February. In monsoon minimum value (123 was found at station II in July and maximum (189) at station II in September. In winter the minimum value (261) was found at station I in October, while maximum (276.3) was found at station II in January.

During the two years study period higher total alkalinity values were observed in winter followed by summer and monsoon.

Free carbon dioxide (mg/l)

Station wise monthly values of free carbon dioxide are given in Table 4.17 and 4.18.

Table 4.17: Monthly values of Carbon dioxide (mg/l) (Year 2007-08)

Stn.	Oct.	Nov.	Dec.	Jan.	Feb.	Mar.	Apr.	May	June	July	Aug.	Sept.
I	–	–	–	–	–	–	–	–	–	–	–	–
II	–	–	0.7	–	–	–	–	–	–	–	–	–
III	–	–	–	–	–	–	–	–	–	–	–	–

Table 4.18: Monthly values of Carbon dioxide (mg/l) (Year 2008-09)

Stn.	Oct.	Nov.	Dec.	Jan.	Feb.	Mar.	Apr.	May	June	July	Aug.	Sept.
I	0.3	–	–	–	–	–	–	–	–	–	–	–
II	–	–	–	0.4	–	–	–	–	–	–	–	–
III	0.2	–	–	–	–	–	–	–	–	–	–	–

In the first year (2007-2008), the free carbon dioxide ranged from Nil to 0.7 mg/l. It was found to be absent for 11 months. It was recorded at station II in December 2007.

In second year (2000-2001), the free carbon dioxide was totally absent from November to December 2008 and February to September 2009. The maximum carbon dioxide (0.4 mg/l) was recorded in January 2009 at station II.

Chlorides (mg/l)

Monthly chloride values of water samples from the three stations (I, II and III) are tabulated in Table 4.19 and 4.20.

Table 4.19: Monthly values of Chlorides (mg/l) (Year 2007-08)

Stn.	Oct.	Nov.	Dec.	Jan.	Feb.	Mar.	Apr.	May	June	July	Aug.	Sept.
I	46.6	58.1	66.2	72.4	81.2	86.1	93.2	96.4	33.5	34.2	33.8	36.8
II	46.8	58.4	67.1	73.6	81.3	88.2	92.8	96.2	33.6	34.1	33.9	36.4
III	47.8	58.9	66.8	72.2	82.2	87.4	92.7	96.1	33.8	34.4	34.2	36.3

Table 4.20: Monthly values of Chlorides (mg/l) (Year 2008-09)

Stn.	Oct.	Nov.	Dec.	Jan.	Feb.	Mar.	Apr.	May	June	July	Aug.	Sept.
I	45.6	52.1	63.4	70.0	80.4	91.1	96.0	96.2	35.2	36.8	39.6	41.6
II	45.4	53.2	64.8	70.2	80.1	90.0	96.2	96.4	37.5	38.3	39.4	41.2
III	46.0	53.6	64.6	70.4	80.8	91.6	96.1	96.9	36.6	38.2	39.8	41.7

Monthly chloride values at three sampling stations in the first year (2007-2008) were 89.2, 89.4 and 89.6 in summer, 34.5, 34.5 and 34.7 in monsoon and 60.8, 61.4 and 61.4 in winter.

In 2008-2009, the mean values of chloride at the stations I, II and III were 91.9, 90.6 and 91.3 in summer, 38.3, 39.3 and 39 in monsoon, and 57.7, 58.4 and 58.6 in winter. During this period, the seasonal maximum and minimum values were 96.9 at spot III in May and 80.1 at station II in February (summer), 41.7 at III in September and 35.2 at station I in June (monsoon) and maximum at 70.4 at station III in January in and minimum at 45.4 at II in October (Winter).

To summarise, during the investigation the study higher values of chlorides were recorded in summer and lower in rainy season.

Total Hardness (mg/l)

Table 4.21 and 4.22 presents station wise and month-wise values of Total Hardness for two-year study period.

Table 4.21: Monthly values of Total hardness (mg/l) (Year 2007-08)

Stn.	Oct.	Nov.	Dec.	Jan.	Feb.	Mar.	Apr.	May	June	July	Aug.	Sept.
I	117	99	133.4	132.4	154	208	206	204	125	130.1	137.4	139.2
II	128	96	132.2	133.6	152.4	210	209	202	124	130.8	141	152
III	113	111	132.4	133.8	156	199	208	210	124.5	130.9	136.2	132.4

Table 4.22: Monthly values of Total hardness (mg/l) (Year 2008-09)

Stn.	Oct.	Nov.	Dec.	Jan.	Feb.	Mar.	Apr.	May	June	July	Aug.	Sept.
I	114.6	120	130	138	184.8	190.1	191.2	207.8	131	133	135	132.8
II	115	121	129	138.4	187.4	190.4	192	208	131.5	132	138	133.4
III	114.4	121.2	128.8	139	185.2	189	190	209	131.8	133.4	137	132

During the first year (2007-2008) the seasonal mean total hardness values at 3 stations (I, II & III) were 193.3, 193.3 and 193.2 (summer), 132.9, 136.9 and 132.9 (monsoon) and 120.4, 122.4 and 122.5 (winter). During this period minimum value (152.4) was recorded at station II in February and maximum (210) was found at station III in May (summer). Similarly minimum values (124) were found at station II in June and maximum (152) at station II in September (monsoon), and minimum (96) was recorded at station III in November and maximum 133.8 was found at station III in January (winter).

During summer of this year while the maximum total hardness (209) was found at station III in May, its minimum (153) was recorded at station I in February. In monsoon the maximum total hardness (138) was found at station II in August and minimum (131) was recorded at station I in June and in winter the maximum (139) was found at station III in January, minimum (114.4) was recorded at station III in October.

The higher values of total hardness were recorded during summer and lower values were recorded during the winter season.

DISCUSSION

Temperature is the single most important physical factor controlling the life of a cold-blooded animal. Temperature is critical in growth, reproduction and sometimes survival. Each species of fish has an optimum temperature range for growth, as well as upper and lower lethal temperatures. Below the optimum temperature feed consumption and feed conversion decline until a temperature is reached at which growth ceases and feed consumption is limited to a maintenance ration. Below this temperature is a lower lethal temperature at which death occurs. Above the optimum temperature feed consumption increases while feed conversion declines.

The maximum and minimum temperatures of reservoir water were observed in the months of May and October respectively. The values ranged between 17 to 32° C. Steady change in the atmospheric temperature with the change in the seasons results in the corresponding change in the water temperature. High summer temperature and bright sunshine accelerate the process of decay of organic matter resulting into the liberation of large quantities of CO_2 and nutrients (Agarwal and Rajwar, 2010).

Reservoirs having water temperature more than 22° C are the highly productive reservoirs (Jhingran and Sugunan, 1990; Sugunan 1995). The average water temperature was recorded at 24.93° C, and 24.71° C during first and second year of the investigation, which reveal that Harni (Katgaon) reservoir is highly productive. During the present study air and water temperatures followed a common pattern; it was high in summer and relatively lower in monsoon and winter. Such type of observations were made by Sakhare (2007). The highest temperature recorded in summer months can be attributed to the direct relationship between bright sunshine, its duration and air temperature in the tropical countries (Hussain, 1977).

Water temperature plays an important role in either decreasing or increasing the concentration of certain chemical characteristics of water. The occurrence of aquatic organisms of a given water body is also directly or indirectly linked with the variation in temperature ranges.

Khatri (1985) recorded the water temperature hat varied from a minimum of 21.8° C to 26° C in Idukki reservoir of Kerala, which is almost similar to the observations made in the present investigation.Kiran and Puttaiah (2010) also recorded water temperature of Bhadra reservoir of Karnataka in the range of 23 to 30.5° C.

pH is measure of the relative acidity of the water. The pH in a pond fluctuates daily due to uptake and release of CO_2 during photosynthesis and respiration. The pH is lowest at or mear dawn and highest at mid-afternoon. The desirable range of early morning pH for from 6.5 to 9.0.The acid death point is a pH of approximately 4 and the alkaline death point is approximately pH 11.When the pH is outside the desirable range, fish growth is slowed, reproduction reduced and susceptibility to disease increased.

The pH is affected not only by the reaction of carbon dioxide but also by organic and inorganic solutes present in water. Any alteration in water pH is accompanied by the change in other physico-chemical parameters. pH maintenance (buffering capacity) is one of the most important attributes of any aquatic system since all the biochemical activities depend on pH of the surrounding water. In the present study, the range of pH on the study sites was between 6.5 to 8.5. pH increased during summer months. Maximum values during summer may be due to increased photosynthesis of the algal blooms resulting into the precipitation of carbonates of calcium and magnesium-from bicarbonates causing higher alkalinity. The decrease in pH during monsoon may be due to greater inflow of water (Agarwal and Rajwar, 2010).

Das (1961) reported that pH of water has an important behavior on both plankton and microbial production. He found that a pH ranging between 7.2 to 8.5 was favourable for the growth of plankton and higher values were detrimental to plankton production, microbial production and thereby to the fish production also.

In the present study the water pH ranged between 6.5 to 8.5. The water was alkaline throughout the study period. This observation is similar to the investigation made by Charak and Fayaz (2006) on Salal reservoir in Jammu and Kashmir (7.4 to 8.5). The present findings also corroborate with findings of Sakhare (2005) which mentions the pH values of 8.1 to 8.6 in Hingni (Pangaon) reservoir of Solapur district (Maharashtra).

A large number of investigations (Nees 1946; Hutchinson 1957) studied the pH of the water body relation to fish growth and observed that largest yields were obtained from water which was just on the alkaline side of neutrality between pH 7.0 to 8.0.

According to Banerjea (1967), water with an almost neutral reaction with pH 6.5 to 7.5 is best suited for fish production and an average production is expected in the pH range of 7.5 to 8.5, but Sahi and Sinha (1969) found no relationship of pH of water with pond or lake productivity. The pH values of water in the afternoon are almost always higher than those in the morning due to photosynthesis and respiratory activities of various organisms in the water (Dewan 1973 and Michael 1969).

Water pH in a water bodies might be dependent on its plankton content. Thus, many investigators (Das and Srivastava 1956, Bhowmik 1968 and Mandal 1972) reported that high pH was related to heavy blooms of phytoplankton, while low pH indicates a rise in zooplankton. A slightly alkaline water pH was optimum not only for the fish, but also for fish food organisms. Thus, Michael (1969) observed that when pH ranged between 7.3 to 8.4, the water provided optimum conditions for the growth of plankton.

Optimal growth and survival of aquatic plants and animals require that their environment pH should be confined with a very short range below or above which they will be subjected to various kinds of stresses, and the diurnal fluctuation of pH of a water body should remain in the range of 6.4 to 8.5 in order to support the optimum fish growth (Das, 1996). The average pH value (7.5) of Harni (Katgaon) reservoir is suitable for optimum fish growth.

Water transparency has a significant role in light attenuation with depth, affecting productivity. Reservoirs with rocky and gravel catchment such as those in Jammu and Kashmir, Himachal Pradesh and Jharkhand have deeper euphotic zones of more than 2 m (Vass and Sugunan, 2009). In these reservoirs the temporal variation in transparency is very wide unlike Madhya Pradesh reservoirs (Unni, 1985). As the reduced transparency in these reservoirs is due to suspended inorganic particles and phytoplankton production is much less, unlike reservoirs with high phytoplankton growth limiting light penetration. Normally the transparency of water decreases during the monsoon due to inflow being loaded with dissolved and suspended organic and inorganic particles, subsequently stabilising in the post-monsoon period (Vass and Sugunan, 2009). In Harni (Katgaon) reservoir maximum transparency was recorded in summer and minimum in rainy season.

In the present investigation at first station the dissolved oxygen was found to range between 4.3 to 9.8 mg/l during the year 2007-2008 and 4.4 to 9.8 mg/l in 2008-2009 and found highest during monsoon. At second station the dissolved oxygen was ranging between 4.3 to 9.8 mg/l in 2007-2008 and 4.2 to 9.7 mg/l in 2008-2009 and found highest during monsoon, while at station III the dissolved oxygen was in the range of 4.1 to 9.7 mg/l and 4.2 to 9.6 mg/l in 2007-2008 and 2008 -2009 respectively with the maximum value during monsoon period.

The minimum concentration of dissolved oxygen recorded in February (4.3 mg/l) and may (4.4 mg/l) in 2008 and 2009 respectively at station I and II, where as in case of station II and III, the minimum concentration of dissolved oxygen 4.3 and 4.1 was observed in April 2008, while during 2009 the minimum dissolved oxygen levels at station II and III were recorded at 4.2 and 4.3 mg/l in month of May.

The average values of dissolved oxygen were 7.19 and 7.62 mg/l during 2007-2008 and 2008-2009 respectively at station I. At station II the values were 7.26 and 7.45 during year 2008 and 2009 respectively, while in station III the values were 7.19 and 7.44 during year 2007-2008 and 2008-2009.

The oxygen content of water bodies is one of the important parameters in water quality assessment. Its presence is essential in aquatic ecosystems to keep the organisms in balance. It also affects the solubility and availability of many nutrients, hence the productivity of an aquatic ecosystem (Wetzel 1983). Gautam *et al* (2007) observed dissolved oxygen in the range of 3.3 to 7.3 mg/l. Oxygen content is poor during periods of high temperature such as summer season (Pearsall 1921; Bhowmik 1968 and

Chakrabarti 1980), while it is high in winter due to low water temperature (Reid 1961; Moitra and Bhattacharya 1965 and Chakrabarti 1980).

Attempts were made to correlate the oxygen content with the volume of plankton of the water body, and it was observed that the phytoplankton peak corresponds to the high oxygen values (Das and Srivastava 1956; Moitra and Bhattacharya 1965 and Mandal 1972), while the zooplankton peaks are associated with low oxygen values (Das and Srivastava 1956). Studies on the optimum range of dissolved oxygen below 3.0 ppm indicates the possibility of asphyxia due to oxygen deficiency and a minimum of 5 ppm of oxygen is required for a productive fish pond (Banerjea 1967).On the other hand, very high concentration of dissolved oxygen may be lethal to fish fry during the rearing spawn in nursery ponds (Alikunhi 1952).

The higher values of dissolved oxygen in monsoon season may be due to the surficial water of the reservoir was subjected to wind generated turbulence and resultant mixing of surface and subsurface water layers. Thus during monsoon months these establishes an oxygen equilibrium between the water and air. This is not disturbed by the vertical gradient of phytoplankton or bacterial populations. Devi (1997) also gave similar explanation for the fluctuations of dissolved oxygen.

The dissolved oxygen content of warm water fish habitats should not be less than 5 mg/l; during at least 16 hours of any 24 hour period. It may be less than 5 mg/l for a period of not exceeding 8 hours within any 24-hour period and at no time shall the dissolved oxygen content be less than 3 mg/l (Boyd, 1982).The dissolved oxygen range of Harni (Katgaon) water passes all the conditions indicating the good water quality with respect to oxygen content for fish survival.

Highly productive water should have a dissolved oxygen concentration of more than 5 mg/l (Vass and Sugunan,

2009). However, a very high concentration of dissolved oxygen leading to super saturation may become lethal to fish fry, as has been seen in some reservoirs predominantly infested with Microcystis blooms.

Sakhare (2007) reported the range of dissolved oxygen in Yeldari reservoir of Maharashtra which ranged from 6.0 to 14.8 mg/l. The present findings corroborate with Sakhare (2007).

Many workers (Adwant 1989, Khabade and Mule 2010, Patil and Kulkarni 2010, Fokmare and Musaddiq 2005 and Shastri 2005) have discussed the seasonal fluctuations in the dissolved oxygen content of various water bodies in Maharashtra.

The dissolved oxygen ranged from 3.41 to 6.21 mg/1 in Seetadwar lake (Tewari and Mishra, 2005), from 5.30 to 9.00 mg/1 in Deoria tal (Rawat and Sharma, 2005) and from 3.00 to 6.00 mg/1 in Kandhar dam (Surve *et al.*, 2005). Thus, the dissolved oxygen varies greatly from one water body to the other.

Kiran and Puttaiah (2010) recorded 1.40 to 9.52 mg/l of dissolved oxygen in Bhadra reservoir of Karnataka. A reduction in the content of dissolved oxygen during summer months in all the stations could be attributed to higher temperature and increased process of microbial decomposition.

Total alkalinity is the sum of titratable bases in water. In most waters, bicarbonate and carbonate are the predominant bases that contribute to alkalinity. Aquatic animals thrive in waters over a wide range of total alkalinities and do not have a specific requirement for 'alkalinity'. Nevertheless, certain physiological and environmental benefits accure from the presence of ample alkalinity in waters used to raise aquatic animals. These benefits include buffering of water against changes in pH, enhanced natural fertility of waters, and decreased potential for metal toxicity.

The total alkalinity of waters ranges from less than 5 to over 500 mg/l as $CaCO_3$ and is determined by the geology of the aquifer or watershed. Bicarbonate and carbonate are derived primarily from the dissolution of basic minerals. Rivers and lakes in geological regions dominated by silicate rocks and acidic topsoils will have poorly mineralized waters with low alkalinities.

Total alkalinity is an important environmental variable in aquaculture because it interacts with other variables that affect the health of aquatic animals or the fertility of the ecosystem (Boyd and Tucker, 2009).

During the two years study period higher total alkalinity values were observed in winter followed by summer and monsoon.

Chloride is one of the important indicators of pollution. Chlorides are generally present in natural water. The presence of chloride in natural water can be attributed to dissolution of salt deposits, discharges of effluents from chemical industries; oil well operation and sewage discharge. High chlorides content recorded in summer and relatively low values recorded in post monsoon. Similar observations are also made by Mazher Sultana and Jayaraj (2007) and Ganesan and Mazer Sultana (2009).

In the present investigation values of chlorides ranged between 34.1 to 96.9 mg/l. Similar range of chlorides was recorded by Piska *et al.* (2000) and Sakhare (2007). In the first year of the study the higher values were recorded in summer and lower in monsoon. High values of chlorides in summer could be due to their correlation as a result of evaporative water loss. Lower values in monsoon could be attributed to dilution effect and renewal of water mass after summer stagnation.

Total hardness is the sum of the concentrations of calcium and magnesium in water. Total hardness is an aggregate property and cannot be precisely interpreted in relation to aquatic animal health or culture system management unless the concentrations of substances contributing to total hardness are known. The total hardness of natural waters ranges from less than 5 to over 10,000 mg/l as $CaCO_3$.The geology of the aquifer or watershed determines the total hardness and the relative concentrations of calcium and magnesium in fresh waters. Most inland surface waters have total hardness values ranging from less than 5 to 200 mg/l as $CaCO_3$.

Most freshwater animals grow well over a wide range of total hardness values but they may be more susceptible to adverse water quality conditions when hardness values (particularly calcium concentrations) are low. Total hardness values are also generally correlated with native fertility of freshwater systems.

During present investigation the higher values of total hardness were recorded during summer and lower values during the winter season.

Plankton Diversity

INTRODUCTION

The plankton community is a hetergenous group of tiny plants (phytoplankton) and animals (zooplankton) adapted to suspension in the sea and freshwaters. The first use of the term 'plankton' is attributed to the German marine biologist, Victor Hensen. According to Hensen's (1887) terminology 'plankton' included all organic particles 'which float and involuntarily in the open water, independent of shores and bottom'. The dependence of plankton upon water movements for maintenance and transport is accurately implied in this definition (Greek planktos meaning wandering).

The ability of water to produce plankton depends on many factors, but the most important is usually the availability of inorganic nutrients for phytoplankton growth. Essential elements for phytoplankton growth include C, O, P, N, S, K, Na, Ca, Mg, Fe, Mn, Cu, Zn, B, Co, Cl and possibly few others.Phoshprous is the most often element regulating phytoplankton growth.

To monitor the aquatic ecosystems and integrity of water, plankton has been used recently as bioindicator

(Beaugrand *et al.*, 2000). Bioindicators and biotic indexes are being used by Europeans to assess water quality of water bodies (Sousa *et al.*, 2008) for last 100 years.

Phytoplankton community comprises of a heterogeneous group of tiny plants adapted to various aquatic environments. Their nature and distribution varies considerably with respect to seasons and water quality. Their dominance also leads to qualitative changes of aquatic ecosystems. Information pertaining to the nature, type and distribution of these organisms provide clue regarding the environmental conditions prevailing in their habit.

Phytoplankton constitutes the base of the ecological pyramid providing food energy for the higher trophic levels of the aquatic ecosystems. In view of this relationship, attempts have been made to correlate primary productivity and fish yields (e.g. Sreenivasan 1964, 1968;Melack 1979). In addition, phytoplankton is also important as an index of the trophic status of a water body. Thunmark and Nygaard (in Wetzel, 1975) have developed a number of phytoplankton indices to quantify algal species as indicators of aquatic enrichment. Relationship between algal associations and lake fertility is also discussed in detail by Hutchinson (1967).

Various ecological aspects of phytoplankton have been a subject of study in India by several workers (Singh 1979, Hosmani and Bharathi 1980, Nandan and Patel 1985a, 1986, Nandan and Ansari 1999, Khare 1999, Nandan and Jain 2005, Nandan and Mahajan 2006, Ranjan *et al.* 2007 Sivakumar and Karuppasamy 2008, Dhavale *et al.* 2009, Mohite and Joshi 2009, Nasare *et al.* 2009).

Zooplankton communities play an important role in the aquatic food chain and also contribute significantly to the secondary productivity of freshwater ecosystem (Saikia and Das, 2003). It also helps in biomonitoring the freshwater ecosystems (Sinha, 2002). The diversity indices for zooplankton can be used for monitoring freshwater pollution by adopting appropriate diversity measures of species (Saikia and Das, 2003).

Zooplankton by their heterotrophic activity plays a key role in the cycling of organic materials in aquatic ecosystems and used as bioindicators. The biondicators are evaluated through presence/absence, condition, relative abundance, reproductive success, community structure (i.e. composition and diversity), community function (i.e. trophic structure), or any combination thereof (Hellawell, 1986).

Zooplankton supports the economically important fish population. They are the major mode of energy transfer between phytoplankton compositions, abundance and seasonal variations is helpful in planning and successful fishery management (Jhingran, 1974).

Zooplankton can also play an important role in indicating the presence or absence of certain species of fishes or in determining the population densities.

Potentiality of zooplankton as bioindicator is very high because their growth and distribution are dependent on some abiotic (e.g., temperature, salinity, stratification, pollutants) and biotic parameters (e.g., food limitation, predation, competition). Pandey and Verma (2004) revealed that abiotic parameters (e.g., pH, transparency, temperature, dissolved oxygen and some micronutrients) in relation to seasonal fluctuation influence zooplankton abundance.

Protozoa are thought to be the first animals to have evolved. Though they depict remarkable diversity in form and structure, yet they have a simple body consisting only of one cell. All the multicellular organisms are believed to have originated from them. Planktonic protozoans are limited to ciliates and flagellates. Among the unicellular protozoa, the heterotrophic nanoflagellates are the major consumers of free-living bacteria and other smaller heterotrophic nanoflagellates. The abundant heterotrophic nanoflagellates (105 to 108 /L in highly eutrophic lentic ecosystems) range in size from about 1.0 to about 20 Lm. They include non-pigmented species that structurally have very closely related pigmented species in the phytoplankton.

The ciliates are larger in size (8 Lm to 300 Lm) but are less abundant (102 to 104/l). While the smallest planktonic ciliates feed on the picoplankton, the larger ciliates feed on the heterotrophic nanoflagellates and small nanophytoplankton. Among the ciliates, those containing captured chloroplasts from the ingested algae or those containing more permanent symbiotic green algae (zoochlorellae) are common. Among the protozoans are two orders of amoebae that are primarily associated with the sediments and littoral aquatic vegetation and large numbers of meroplanktonic species (Edmondson, 1959; Battish, 1992).

Rotifers occur in an endless variety of aquatic and semi-aquatic habitats. These fascinating creatures were first studied and described by Leeuwenhoek as early as 1703. In the twentieth century Jennings (1903, 1928), De Beauchamp (1928, 1932), Myers (1931, 1933, 1941), Pennak (1940, 1953) ND Hyman (1940, 1951) made valuable contributions to our knowledge of rotifera. The occurrence and distribution of the rotifers in India has been worked out by several limnologists (Santhanam and Murthy 1985, Anderson 1889, Arora 1962, 1963a, 1964, 1965, 1966a, Nayar 1964, 1965a, 1965b, 1968, Dhanapathi 1973, 1974, 1975b, 1976a, 1976b, 2000; Chowdhary e*t al.* 1978 and Battish 1968, Pradhan *et al.* 2006).

The cladocerans commonly known as 'waterfleas' form a primitive group of microcrustaceans. They invariably constitute a dominant component of freshwater zooplankton, play an important role in the aquatic food chain and also contribute significantly to zooplankton dynamics and secondary productivity in freshwater ecosystems.

Cladocera have been reported from all over the world. While it is true that several genera and some species are cosmopolitan, certain species are endemic. In view of the cosmopolitan nature of this group particularly at the higher taxonomic categories, treatises from the different parts of the world are of importance for any detailed work. In this context, general compilations of Baird (1850), Keilhack (1909),

Henry (1822), Manuilova (1964) and Flossner (1972) are relevant. In the Indian context the studies on cladocera usually form part of general limnological investigations in lakes, ponds and reservoirs, where from several genera and species are reported from time to time. For want of treatises on the Indian species based on well illustrated figures and keys, many errors have crept in. The indiscriminate and uncritical use of monographs from other parts of the world has led to reports of the occurrence of several species that have no place in our fauna. While there are occasional papers on the taxonomy of freshwater cladocera in India, no comprehensive treatment of this group exists for country.

Of the 11 families listed under the order cladocera, nine are known from Indian waters (Michael and Sharma, 1988). The systematic studies on cladocera were initiated as early as 1860,when Baird described a new species of Genus Daphnia from the material collected by Rev. Hislop from Nagpur, Central India.

Cladocerans are a crucial group among zooplankton and form the most useful and nutritive group of crustaceans for higher members of fishes in the food chain.

Copepods are minute (0.3 to 2.5 mm) crustacean lacking a distinct shell fold and having a simple median eye. In their free living forms the body is elongated and segmented, distinguished into a broad appendage-bearing part called the metasoma and posterior urosome separated by a major articulation. The urosome ends in a caudal furca. Of the antennae, the first are often longer and uniramous. The maxillipeds are the first thoracic appendages, followed by four biramous swimming legs with the fifth leg reduced and uniramous. Gravid females carry their eggs in one or two egg sacs. Copepods pass through a series of naupliar and copepoid stages during their development. The copepods comprise of calanoids, cyclopoids and harpacticoids.

Copepods are much hardier and strongly motile than all other zooplankton with their tougher exoskeleton and longer and stronger appendages. They have long developmental time and a complex life history with early larval stages difficult to distinguish. They are almost wholly carnivorous on the smaller zooplankton for their food needs. Among the three orders of copepods, cyclopoid copepods are generally predatory on (carnivorous) on other zooplankton, and fish larvae. The cyclopoid copepods also feed on algae, bacteria and detritus. The second group of copepods, calanoid copepods change their diet with age, sex, season, and food availability. The calanoid copepods are omnivorous feeding on ciliates, rotifers, algae, bacteria and detritus. The third group harpacticoid copepods are primarily benthic.

The Ostracods are bivalved organisms and belong to phylum Arthropoda. They mainly inhabit the lake bottom and among macrophytes and feed on detritus and dead plankton. Ostracods are in turn consumed by fishes and benthic macroinvertebrates (Chakrapani *et al.*1996). There are over 1700 species of known ostracods of which about one-third are freshwater forms. They inhibit a wide variety of freshwaters likes lakes, pools, swamps, streams and heavily polluted areas (Edmondson, 1959).

Multi-lake studies have been used to explore variations in the zooplankton community along a number of limnological gradients. For example, zooplankton community size structure has been used as an indicator of lake trophic status (Bays and Crisman, 1983, Beaver and Crisman, 1990, Canfield and Jones, 1996 and Pace, 1986). Studies have compared the abundance and biomass of micro- and macrozooplankton (Bays and Crisman, 1983, Pace, 1986 and Sprules *et al.* 1988) to algal chlorophylls (Canfield and Jones, 1996), Carlson's Trophic State Index (Bays and Crisman, 1983), and nutrients (Pace, 1986 and Sprules, 1977). Zooplankton indicator species have been used to determine shifts in trophic state (e.g., Fuller *et al.*1977 and Sprules, 1977). Several studies have examined differences in rotifer communities in lakes of various trophic states (Beaver and Crisman, 1990, Fuller *et al.* 1977 and Gannon and Stemberger, 1978). Abundance of selected major zooplankton groups (e.g. Rotifera, Copepoda) has also been used to show changes in trophic state (Gannon and Stemberger, 1978 and Pace, 1986).

The zooplankton study has been a fascinating subject for a long time. Enough literature exists on the plankton of various water bodies (Arora 1966, Victor and Fernando *et al.*, 1982, Chauhan 1988, Kulshrestha *et al.* 1989, Fasihuddin and Kumari 1990, Kumar 1995, Singh and Sinha 1995, Sinha and Sinha 1993, Choudhary and Singh 1999, Maruthanayagam *et al.* 2003, Sahib 2004, Sunkad and Patil 2004, Mishra 2005, Chandrasekhar 2006, Chavan *et al.* 2006, Thirumathal 2006, Mukherji and Nandi 2006, Renuga and Ramnibai 2006, Kiran *et al.* 2007, Rawat and Sharma 2010). Such studies from state of Maharashtra have been very recently initiated and the only contributions on this aspect are those of Deshmukh (2001) Pandit *et al.* (2007), Harney *et al.* (2008), Pawar *et al.* (2003), Sakhare (2007), Sakhare and Joshi (2002, 2006) and Goel *et al.* (1968).

MATERIALS AND METHODS

Standard methodology after Welch (1948) and Jhingran *et al* (1969), with suitable modifications to suit local availability was used. Procedure adopted is briefly described below:

(a) Collection

(b) Preservation and transportation

(c) Washing

(d) Qualitative analysis

(e) Quantitative analysis

(a) *Collection:* Collection of planktons was done by using a plankton net with 38 cm diameter of the mouth and a bolting silk No. 20 (173 meshes/inch). An inron tube was firmly tied to the tapering end of the net and the open end of the plankton collecting tube was covered by a piece of bolting silk, securely tied with cotton thread so that plankton collected through the net could be easily transferred into separate plastic bottles.

(b) *Preservation and transportation:* Initial study for taxonomic identification and general behaviour was carried out on live plankton. Subsequently; quantitative estimations were made on plankton preserved in 5% formalin. An ice container was used for live transportation to the laboratory.

(c) *Washing:* Samples collected from Harni (Katgaon) reservoir were easily washed with formalin water. For this purpose a glass funnel and a piece of bolting silk were used. But, washing was rather difficult for samples collected from few sites. It is because these samples contained lot of debris, micro and macro-phytes. By using a wash bottle containing formalin water, washing was carried out in the following manner:

The whole plankton sample was measured (used for quantitative estimation) and diluted to a desirable concentration depending upon the density of plaktonic population in such a way that they could be easily counted individually under light binocular microscope. For dilution a polson plankton splitter was used. Generally one fourth of the total biomass in a sample was used for washing to minimize error. This small fraction of collected plankton material was transferred on a set of different mesh size sieves and shaken gently. By this procedure, it was possible to remove easily the fine debris and soil particles. After that, the whole plankton material was collected in Petri-plate containing formalin water. At this stage, the sample containing some plant material and some other foreign particles were easily removed with the help of different size brushes. Finally, the remaining plankton material was transferred to fresh formalin solution and the whole plankton concentration was measured and multiplied with the dilution factor, already made by splitter.

(d) *Qualitative Analysis:* For qualitative analysis, a light binocular and an inverted plankton microscope are used. As far as possible, the animals were identified up to species level.

Preliminary identification was made by using Pennak (1978), Battish (1992), Michael (1973) and Dhanapathi (2000) as basic references.

The rotifers were ordinarily distinguished at species level by trophic characteristics in whole animal. Although in some difficult cases animals were crushed with the help of 2 micro-needles to force animal out.

Generally, the cladocerans were identified by carapace characteristics, although in a number of cases a minor dissection of post abdominal segment with the help of 2 mico-needles was carried out. After dissection, these abdominal segments were observed under high power in a glycerine mount.

Copepods were generally identified with the help of body appendages and for species identification a minor dissection on the 5th leg was carried out in a glycerine mount. Animal or dissected apart as observed under high power.

For identification of ostracods, body shell was removed to study detailed structure. These animals also required a minor dissection of furca. After dissection, furca was observed under high power in glycerine.

(e) *Quantitative Estimation:* For quantitative estimation of plankton, a Sedgwick-Rafter counting cell of mm^2 and micropipette of glass van grade I of 1, 2 and 5 ml capacity were used. For this purpose, 1 ml of plankton sample was drawn and transferred to the Sedgwick-Rafter counting cell. Observations were made under the binoculars and counting was done up to genetic level. For the sake of convenience, blood cell counter make was used for accurate and quick counting. The procedure was repeated 5 times to get an average. The total population of individual plankton genera in a reservoir was calculated by the following formula:

$N = n \times 1/w$

Where,

N= Number of individuals of a species per cubic meter

n= Number of individuals of a species in 1 ml.

1= Dilution factor

w= Amount of water hauled

When the plankton were collected by filtration the pollution of a species was calculated as follows:

N= n×d×10/w

Where,

N= Number of individuals of a species in cubic meter

n= Average number of individual of a species in one ml

d= Dilution factor

w= Amount of water filtered.

RESULTS

ZOOPLANKTON DIVERSITY

During 2007-08, rotifer dominated the zooplankton population (40.80%), followed by copepoda (23.74%), cladocera and ostracoda (12.92% each) and protozoa (9.7%). The percentage composition of zooplankton during year 2007-08 is presented in figure 5.1. Total 34 different species of zooplankton were identified (Table 5.1). The maximum zooplankton population was observed during summer and minimum during winter season (Fig. 5.2).

Protozoans were high in rainy season. Rotifers, cladocerans, copepods as well as ostracods showed the summer maxima. The protozoans, ostracods,rotifers and copepods showed minima in winter season, while cladocerans were observed less in rainy season.

Protozoans were represented by 6 species (Table 5.2). The species *Paramecium caudatum* and *Colpidium sps* were observed in 10 months, while *Opercularia sps* and *Arcella sps* were absent in rainy summer season respectively. *Difflugia* and *Vortocella sps* were absent for the months of summer

(February and March). The maximum protozoan population was recorded in August 2008 (73 organisms /liter) and minimum population in the month of November 2007 (17 organisms/liter).

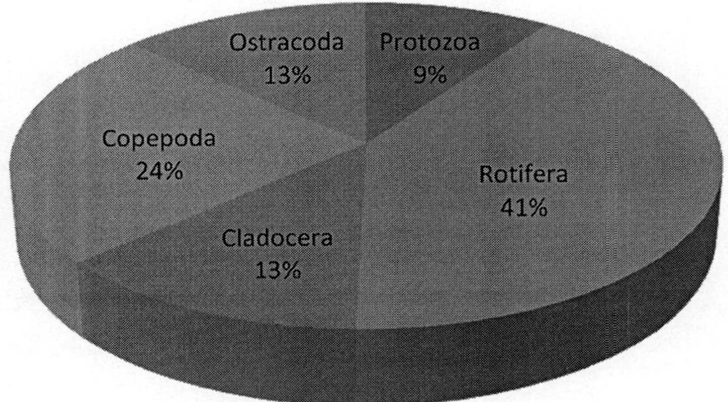

Fig.5.1: The percentage of composition of zooplankton in Harni (Katgaon) reservoir during 2007-08

Table 5.1: List of zooplankton in Harni (Katgaon) resevoir

Protozoans: *Diffugia spp* *Arcella spp* *Vorticella spp* *Opercularia spp* *Paramecium caudatum* *Colpidium sp.*
Rotifera: *Branchionus flacatus* *Brachionus calyciflorus* *Brachionus diversicornis* *Filina longiseta* *Keratella tropica* *Keretella quadrata* *Lecane bulla* *Trichocera porecelus* *Trichocera longiseta*

(Table Contd...)

Cladocera:
Indialona ganapati *Moina micrura* *Diaphanosma sarsi* *Alona rectangular* *Biapertura karna* *Ceriodaphnia cornuta* *Diaphanosoma excisum*
Copepoda:
Diaptomus marshianus *Phylladiaptomus anus annae* *Nedodiaptomus linddbergi* *Nauplius larva* *Mesocyclops leukarti* *Mesocyclops hyalinus* *Cyclops viridis*
Ostracoda:
Stenocypris sp *Cypris obensa* *Stenocypris sp* *Cyclocypria globosa* *Candocypria osborni* *Cyprinotus sps.*

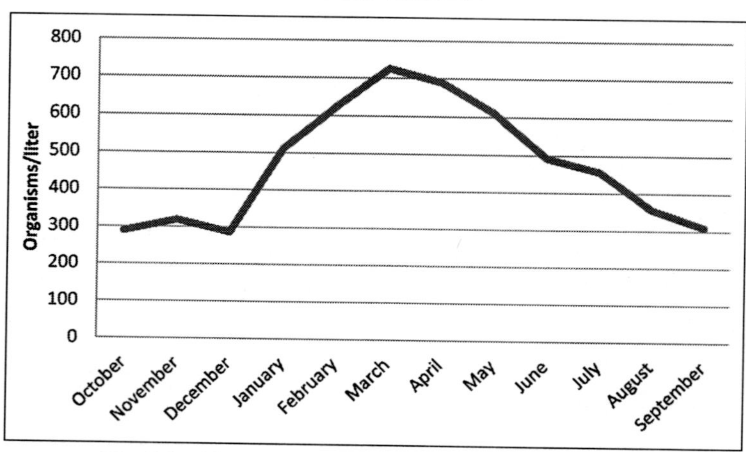

Fig.5.2: Monthly fluctuations in zooplankton in Harni (Katgaon) reservoir during year 2007-08

Table 5.2: Composition of protozoans (density:organisms/ liter) during year 2007-08

	Oct.	Nov.	Dec.	Jan.	Feb.	Mar.	Apr.	May	June	July	Aug.	Sept.
Difflugia Sps.	20	03	09	03	–	–	05	02	03	18	30	21
Arcella Sps.	12	05	07	06	–	–	–	–	10	15	16	12
Voritcella sps.	08	02	02	04	–	–	04	–	05	13	12	13
Opercularia sps.	09	–	03	13	02	06	10	16	–	–	–	–
Paramecium, caudatum	07	03	02	20	18	30	16	18	11	18	13	03
Colpidium sps.	06	04	04	08	04	09	05	07	08	04	02	05

Rotifers were represented by 9 species (Table 5.3) and species *Brachionus flacatus,Brachionus diversicornis* and *Keratella tropica* recorded throughout the study period, while *Lecane bulla* was accounted for 8 months only. The peak of rotifers was observed during months of May 2008 (264 organisms/ liter) and it was minimum in the month of October (100 organisms/liter).

Cladocera were represented by 6 species (Table 5.4). The species *Indialona ganapati, Diaphanosoma sarsi, Ceriodaphnia cornuta* and *Diaphanosoma excisum* were recorded throughout the investigation, while *Alona rectanguila* was totally absent in rainy season. *Moina micrura* and *Biapertura karna* were absent in two months of winter season. The maximum cladoceran population (126 organisms/liter) was recorded during March and minimum population (32 organisms/liter) during November.

Copepoda was represented by 7 species (Table 5.5).The maxima was 207 organisms/liter during March and minima was 54 organisms/liter during December. *Mesocyclops sps* and *Neodiaptomus lindbergi* were accounted throughout the year while *Diaptomus marshianus* was absent in three months of rainy season (July to September). *Nauplius larva* and *Cyclops viridis* were absent in October and December 2007.

Table 5.3: Composition of rotifera (density:organisms/liter) during year 2007-08

	Oct.	Nov.	Dec.	Jan.	Feb.	Mar.	Apr.	May	June	July	Aug.	Sept.
Brachionus falcatus	24	23	32	38	51	46	60	70	63	50	42	38
Brachionus calyciflorus	12	38	–	22	16	21	18	26	30	25	14	24
Brachionus diversicornis	22	22	16	29	38	49	50	40	17	26	15	22
Filinia longiseta	–	19	19	12	19	18	23	20	15	–	05	–
Keratella tropica	21	16	12	10	22	30	24	21	34	27	16	25
Keratella quadrata	11	12	14	16	14	12	22	30	21	22	–	–
Lecane bulla	–	18	18	21	32	29	22	–	19	13	–	–
Trichocera porcelus	10	–	13	24	20	24	22	29	28	20	–	–
Trichocera longiseta	–	14	19	20	21	27	20	28	25	19	20	24

Table 5.4: Composition of cladocera (density:organisms/liter) during year 2007-08

	Oct.	Nov.	Dec.	Jan.	Feb.	Mar.	Apr.	May	June	July	Aug.	Sept.
Indialona ganapati	07	02	07	16	12	19	22	07	07	06	10	07
Moina micrura	06	–	–	18	22	28	18	08	09	09	11	10
Diaphanosoma excisum	09	04	03	14	15	10	04	07	08	04	01	02
Diaphanosoma sarsi	08	09	09	10	14	20	16	05	02	04	06	04
Alona rectangular	04	08	06	17	21	18	13	10	–	–	–	–
Biapertura karna	–	–	07	15	18	22	08	06	06	13	07	06
Ceriodaphnia cornuta	07	09	02	09	16	09	09	04	03	03	02	05

Table 5.5: Composition of copepoda (density:organisms/liter) during year 2007-08

	Oct.	Nov.	Dec.	Jan.	Feb.	Mar.	Apr.	May	June	July	Aug.	Sept.
Diaptomus marshianus	13	15	09	12	18	21	30	22	14	–	–	–
Phyllodiaptomus annae	–	08	05	08	17	20	23	26	16	16	18	–
Neodiaptomus lindbergi	20	12	13	13	27	27	40	22	13	13	08	14
Nauplius larva	–	07	–	15	18	30	25	28	28	11	17	07
Mesocyclops leukarti	11	26	14	20	25	41	31	21	15	23	12	12
Mesocyclops hyalinus	14	08	13	32	42	50	28	18	19	09	16	20
Cyclops viridis	–	11	–	07	11	18	08	29	10	08	07	06

Ostracoda was represented by 5 species (Table 5.6). The highest density of ostracods was observed in April (112 organisms/liter), while lowest density was recorded in November 2007 (21 organisms/liter).

During second year of investigation (2008-09) zooplankton were represented by protozoa, rotifera, cladocera, copepod and ostracoda. The percentage composition of zooplankton during year 2008-09 is presented in figure 5.3. The monthly variation in total plankton population during year 2008-09 is shown in figure 5.4.

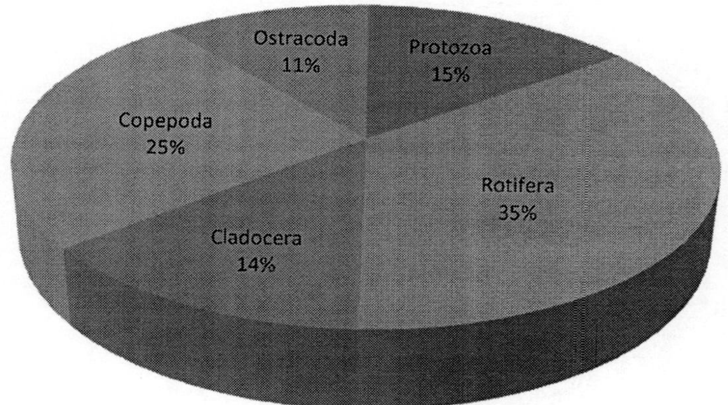

Fig. 5.3: The percentage of composition of zooplankton in Harni (Katgaon) reservoir during 2008-09

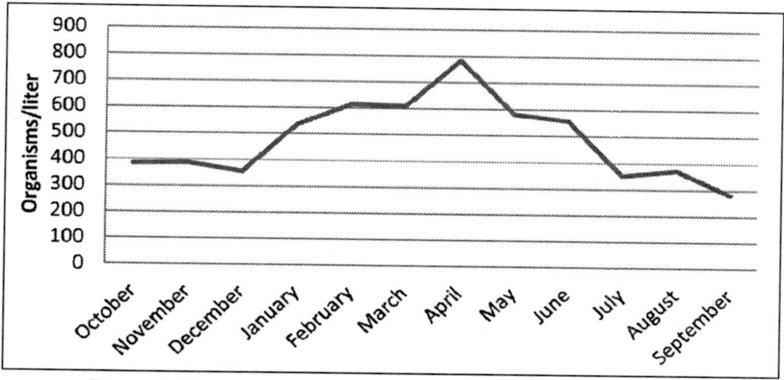

Fig.5.4:Monthly fluctuations in zooplankton in Harni (Katgaon) reservoir during year 2008-09

Table 5.6: Composition of ostracoda (density:organisms/liter) during year 2007-08

	Oct.	Nov.	Dec.	Jan.	Feb.	Mar.	Apr.	May	June	July	Aug.	Sept.
Stenocypris Sps.	–	–	–	12	20	16	27	21	10	15	20	28
Cypris obensa	10	06	10	07	19	18	30	19	09	10	14	03
Cyclocypris globosa	12	07	04	18	22	23	23	22	21	17	13	07
Candocypria osborni	–	03	08	13	19	20	17	17	10	12	–	05
Cyprinotus sps	06	05	06	08	10	13	15	10	12	13	10	07

Protozoa was represented by 6 species (Table 5.7). The maxima was 95 organisms/liter during October and minima was 54 organisms/liter during January 2009. *Vorticella sps* were absent throughout the summer and *Cospidium sps* were present only in 7 months. *Difflugia sps* and *Arcella sps* were also absent in three months of summer.

Rotifera accounted for about 35% during year 2008-09 and were represented by 9 species (Table 5.8). The highest density of rotifers (278 organisms/liter) was recorded in the month of April 2009 and minimum in September 2009 (102 organisms/liter). Throughout the summer months, rotifer population was maximum. It was minimum in rainy season.

Cladocerans accounted for about 14% and were represented by 7 species (Table 5.9). The maximum population was recorded in March (131 organisms/liter) and minimum population in the month of November (37 organisms/liter). Cladocerans were maximum throughout the summer season. Out of 7 species, 5 were present throughout the year, while *Alona rectangular* was absent in rainy season. *Biapertura karna* was not seen in October 2008.

Copepoda was accounted for about 25% and were represented by 7 species (Table 5.10), and *Neodiaptomus lindbergi* was absent throughout the study period. *Diaptomus marshianus* and *Mesoccyclops hyalinus* were present for 8 and 9 months respectively. *Cyclops viridis, Mesocyclops leukarti, Nauplius larva* and *Phylladiaptomus annae* were present in 11 months. The peak period of copepods was observed during month of April (255 organisms/liter) and it was minimum during the month of September 2009 (26 organisms/liter).

Ostracoda was represented by 5 species (Table 5.11). *Cyclocypris globosa* and *Cyprinotus sps* were present for 12 months. *Stenocypris sps* were absent for 3 months of winter season and two months of rainy season. *Cypris obensa* and *Candocyprias osbornii* were absent in two months of rainy season. Throughout the summer month, ostracod population was maximum. It was minimum in rainy season.

Table 5.7: Composition of protozoans (density:organisms/liter) during year 2008-09

	Oct.	Nov.	Dec.	Jan.	Feb.	Mar.	Apr.	May	June	July	Aug.	Sept.
Difflugia Sps.	23	12	08	09	–	–	–	15	20	24	28	20
Arcella Sps.	20	08	20	10	13	–	–	–	13	21	17	30
Voritcella sps.	19	14	08	06	–	–	–	–	10	19	26	18
Opercularia sps.	12	11	12	03	14	09	27	20	18	–	–	–
Paramecium, caudatum	21	16	10	08	23	38	32	23	21	13	–	–
Colpidium sps.	–	–	–	08	13	15	06	16	–	–	06	04

Table 5.8: Composition of rotifera (density:organisms/liter) during year 2008-09

	Oct.	Nov.	Dec.	Jan.	Feb.	Mar.	Apr.	May	June	July	Aug.	Sept.
Brachionus falcatus	28	24	13	35	33	42	56	34	17	21	30	29
Brachionus calyciflorus	–	–	15	17	30	19	26	30	32	15	26	18
Brachionus diversicornis	–	08	19	26	28	39	30	27	30	18	21	24
Filinia longiseta	–	20	–	23	10	08	17	11	16	22	–	–
Keratella tropica	26	25	17	29	25	27	33	25	26	17	25	20
Keratella quadrata	20	15	13	09	14	22	28	29	12	–	–	–
Lecane bulla	21	17	09	20	22	15	30	26	20	14	–	14
Trichocera porcelus	20	15	20	18	14	18	21	06	12	09	–	–
Trichocera longiseta	22	18	21	28	20	28	29	10	22	23	28	–

Table 5.9: Composition of cladocera (density:organisms/liter) during year 2008-09

	Oct.	Nov.	Dec.	Jan.	Feb.	Mar.	Apr.	May	June	July	Aug.	Sept.
Indialona ganapati	08	04	09	17	13	17	25	08	07	08	12	09
Moina micrura	09	10	09	19	20	30	21	14	10	08	13	14
Diaphanosoma excisum	08	03	03	16	18	10	03	04	10	05	02	03
Diaphanosoma sarsi	09	03	03	12	13	18	12	07	03	06	05	03
Alona rectangular	08	06	07	15	25	19	17	12	–	–	–	–
Biapertura karna	–	05	04	17	20	28	11	03	08	14	07	03
Ceriodaphnia cornuta	04	06	04	08	14	19	06	04	02	03	03	07

Table 5.10:Composition of copepoda (density:organisms/liter) during year 2008-09

	Oct.	Nov.	Dec.	Jan.	Feb.	Mar.	Apr.	May	June	July	Aug.	Sept.
Diaptomus marshianus	–	22	10	10	38	30	21	14	28	–	–	–
Phyllodiaptomus annae	–	14	10	21	18	08	20	10	30	12	15	18
Neodiaptomus lindbergi	20	10	20	18	10	20	35	28	26	20	18	08
Nauplius larva	08	08	14	13	19	12	22	15	18	08	20	–
Mesocyclops leukarti	16	12	06	18	32	42	70	40	27	16	22	–
Mesocyclops hyalinus	12	24	18	20	40	10	65	35	22	–	–	–
Cyclops viridis	06	09	15	16	16	15	22	20	20	11	11	–

Table 5.11: Composition of ostracoda (density:organisms/liter) during year 2008-09

	Oct.	Nov.	Dec.	Jan.	Feb.	Mar.	Apr.	May	June	July	Aug.	Sept.
Stenocypris Sps.	–	–	–	06	12	13	30	25	18	10	–	–
Cypris obensa	07	11	05	10	14	16	22	16	22	–	–	11
Cyclocypris globosa	12	10	08	15	13	12	18	10	06	08	10	16
Candocypria osborni	13	09	09	13	11	10	13	28	20	–	08	–
Cyprinotus sps	12	08	11	12	08	10	15	16	12	06	04	08

PHYTOPLANKTON DIVERSITY

10 species of chlorophyceae, 5 species of cyanophyceae, 6 species of bacillariophyceae and 3 species of euglenophyceae were recorded from the Harni (Katgaon) reservoir (Table 5.12).

Table 5.12: Phytoplankton diversity in Harni (Katgaon) reservoir

Chlorophyceae:
Ulothrix zonata
Zygnema sp
Pediastrum duplex,
Pediastrum simplex,
Scendesmus armatus,
Oedogonium patulum,
Ankistrodesmus falcatus,
Chlorella valgoris,
Cosmarium contractum,
Closterium limneticum
Cyanophyceae:
Oscillatoria chlorine
Oscillatoria limnosa
Anabaena constricta
Merismopedia punctata
Microcystis aerugenose
Bacillariophyceae:
Navicula gracilis
Navicula viridula
Nitzschia subtilis
Bacillaria paradoxa
Diatoms vuloare
Synedra affinis
Euglenophyceae:
Eugelna stellata,
Euglena viridis
Euglena pisciformis

From chlorophyceae *Chlorella valgaris, Pediastrum spp* and *Scendesmus armatus* dominated the reservoir. The maximum population of chlorophyceae was recorded in April (1360 l^{-1}).

From cyanophyceae *Oscillatoria spp* and *Microcystis aeurogenose* dominated the reservoir. This group attained a highest peak in summer, with maxima in May at 2010 l^{-1}.

Among bacillariophyceae *Navicula spp,Synedra affinis* and *Bacillaria paradoxa* dominated the reservoir. Their population was maximum (470 l^{-1}) in July. The maximum population of bacillariophyceae in rainy season may be due to the inflow of water inside the reservoir.

Euglenophyceae was represented by 3 species.*Euglema spp* increased in number in winter season. The maximum population of euglenophyceae was recorded in December (540 l^{-1}).

DISCUSSION

Present study has revealed 6 species of protozoans, 9 species of rotifers, 7 species of cladocera, 7 species of copepods and 6 species of ostracoda.

Renuga and Ramanibai (2010) studied the zooplanktonic community of Krishnagiri reservoir in Tamil Nadu. They recorded 23 species of zooplankton belonging to 4 groups i.e., rotifer, cladocera, copepod and ostracoda. Rotifera represented by 8 species, cladocera represented by 5 species, copepod by 6 species and ostracoda by 4 species.

Rajashekhar *et al.* (2010) studied seasonal variation of zooplankton from Khaji kotnar reservoir in Gulbarga district of Karnataka. Out of 24 species, 10 species belongs to rotifer, 6 species belongs to cladocera, 5 species belongs to copepod and 3 species of ostracoda. Rotifera was the dominant group throughout the study period and highest count was recorded in the summer season while low incidence was observed in southwest monsoon season.

Moitra and Bhowmik (1968) observed members of three main zooplanktonic groups i.e., rotifera, cladocera and copepoda, which dominate in freshwater fish pond in Kalyani, West Bengal.

In Ramauna reservoir four genera of rotifera and cladocera and two genera under copepod were observed by Agarwal (1980). However, Pathak and Mudgal (2004) observed five genera of rotifers, three genera of cladocerans and ostracodans and two genera each in respect of protozoans and copepodans in Visla reservoir of Madhya Pradesh.

The numerical variation in peak periods of different group of zooplankton might be due to different biological parameters. In Harni (Katgaon) reservoir rotifers were found dominant over the other groups. This findings is in agreement with Chakravarthy and Asthana (1989), Kohli *et al.* (1982) and Kiran *et al.* (2007).

Sakhare (2007) recorded 8 species of rotifers, 6 species of cladoerans, 7 species of copepods and 4 species of ostracods from Yeldari reservoir in Maharashtra.

Deshmukh (2001) and Sakhare (2007) reported maximum rotifers in summer season, which corroborate with the present investigation.

Cladocerans popularly known as 'water flea' prefer to live in deep water and constitute a major item of food for fish. Thus they hold key position in food chain and energy transformation (Uttangi, 2001). About 6000 species of freshwater cladocerans occur through the world (Korovchinsky, 1996) of which 110 species have been recorded from India (Patil and Goudar, 1989). Pandit *et al.* (2007) observed *Ceriodaphina cornuta, Bosminopsis dietersi, Biapertura karua* and *Alona pulchella* in Pravara river near Sangamner, Maharashtra. Polulation of cladocerans in different water bodies have been reported by Rao and Muley (1981), Kaushik and Sharma (1994), Murugan *et al.* (1998), Mathew (1985) and Battish and Kumari (1986).

Freshwater copepods constitute one of the major zooplankton communities occurring in all types of water bodies and ranging from free living to parasitic forms. They serve as food to several fishes and play a major role in ecological pyramids. About 120 species of the free living freshwater copepods are known from India (Uttangi, 2001).

In the present study, most abundant species of copepods were *Mesocyclops leukarti* and *Neodiaptomus lindbergi*. Chauhan (1993) has recorded maximum copepods in summer and minimum during winter. According to Das *et al.* (1996) copepods favour more stable environment and generally regarded as pollution sensitive taxa as they disappear once a water gets polluted.

Ostracods are small crustaceans having the bivalve carapace enclosing the laterally compressed body. They inhabit all kinds of freshwater and marine water environments. The freshwater ostracods occur in lakes, ponds, pools, swamps, streams and even polluted waters. Majority of them are free living and few are commensals on the gills of cray fishes and in the intestine of fishes and amphibians. Approximately 110 species are known from the inland water bodies of the Indian subcontinent (Patil and Gouder, 1989).

In the present study among ostracods *Stenocypris sps, Cypris obensa, Cyclocypris globosa, Candocypria osborni and Cyprinotus sps* were recorded.

Pandit *et al.* (2007) recorded *Hemicypris fossucula* and *Darwinula sp* from Paravara river. According to Harshey *et al.* (1987) ostracods grow well in hard water. Hujare (2005) reported absence of any seasonal trend in ostracods.

Distribution of phytoplankton and zooplankton in time and space, their composition and seasonal variations are essential pre-requisite for any successful fishery management. The plankton community structure represents the biological productivity of the system.

The phytoplankton in a reservoir is an important biological indicator of the water quality. While phytoplankton are important primary producers and the basis of the food chain in open water, some species on the other hand can be harmful to human and other vertebrates by releasing toxic substances (hepatotoxins or neurotoxins etc.) into the water. Proliferation of harmful organisms, particularly species should be monitored. Phytoplankton studies and monitoring are useful for control of the physico-chemical and biological conditions of the water in any irrigation project. Therefore certain groups of phytoplankton, especially blue green algae, can degraded recreational value of surface water, particularly thick surface scum, which reduces the use of amenities for contact sports, or large concentrations, which cause deoxygenation of the water leading to fish death (Whitton and Patts, 2000). Over the last few decades, there has been much interest in the processes influencing the development of phytoplankton communities, primarily in relation to physico-chemical factors (Akbay *et al.*, 1999; Peerapornpisal *et al.*, 1999; Elliott *et al.*, 2002).

In India, many hydrobiologists have carried out a considerable amount of research on seasonal succession, production, phytoplankton abundance and the variations in the different freshwater ecosystems.

Govind (1963) worked on the phytoplankton functions with reference to environmental condition and factors regulating the production and succession of algae.

Hosmani and Bharthi (1980) carried out limnological studies of ponds and lakes of dharwad with reference to phytoplankton ecology of four waterbodies.

Goel *et al.* (1986) studied the freshwater bodies with special reference to their chemistry and phytoplankton in Southern Maharashtra. Mahajan (2005) studied phytoplankton in a reservoir of Khargone, Madhya Pradesh.

Kant and Raina (1985) studied the qualitative and quantitative distribution of phytoplankton from two ponds of Jammu.

Sharma (2009) recorded 75 species of phytoplankton belonging to six groups from Loktak Lake in Manipur.

Sharma and Lyngdoh (2003) studied abundance and ecology of net and phytoplankton of a subtropical reservoir of Meghalaya (N.E. India).

Venu and Seshavatharam (1984) studied phytoplankton production in relation to physico-chemical conditions in lake Kondakarla.

The qualitative texture of phytoplankton community observed in Harni (Katgaon) reservoir indicated a sequence of chlorophyceae (10)>bacillariophyceae (6)>cyanophyceae (5) and euglenophyceae (3).

Kumar (1995) reported bacillariophyceae, chlorophyceae and cyanophyceae among phytoplankton. Phytoplankton community constituted 64.9 to 66.8 per cent of total zooplankton and showed its peak values in January and September. The members belong to bacillariophyceae (80.5%) and cyanophyceae (87.3%) dominated during January and September respectively.

Yousuf and Parveen (1990) recorded 84 taxa of phytoplankton from Dal lake. Of these 50 belonged to chlorophyceae, 16 each to cyanophyceae and bacillariophyceae and two to euglenophyceae. Chlorophyceae was the most dominant group among the phytoplankton population qualitatively as well as quantitatively. The group contributed on an average about 48.06% of the total population, recording a range of 10.25% to 93.43%. Bacillariophyceae contributed 4.09% to 87.09% with a mean of 26.33%. Eugelnophyceae was next in order contributing on an average 15.22% of the total population. Cyanphyceae was the most scare group with a mean contribution of 10.38%.

Verma and Shukla (1970) recorded 30 genera of phytoplankton from Kamla Nehru tank, Muzzafarnagar.

Similarly Hossain *et al.* (2006) recorded 38 genera of phytoplankton during three month study period in earthen fish ponds within the Mymensingh region of Bangladesh.

Harilal (2005) recorded 23 genera of phytoplankton from Neyyar and 20 from Karamana river of Kerala. Members of chlorophyceae were found to predominate in two rivers.

Ayoade *et al.* (2009) recorded 32 genera of phytoplankton from Tehri dam. Green algae which accounted for 69.5% of the phytoplankton density were represented by 10 genera.

In present investigation the phytoplankton constituted 84.19% of the total plankton, while the zooplankton was recorded at 15.81% of the total plankton (Table 5.13). Sugunan and Yadava (1991b) reported 96.41% of phytoplankton and 3.59% of zooplankton in the Nongmahir reservoir of Meghalaya. In Yeldari reservoir Sakhare (2007) recorded 84.03% phytoplankton and 15.97% zooplankton.

Table 5.13: Plankton groups and their composition in Harni (Katgaon) reservoir during year 2007-09

Groups	Range (Units l^{-1})	Average (%)
Chlorophyceae	370 to 1360	1060 (34.99)
Cyanophyceae	420 to 2010	910 (30.04)
Bacillariophyceae	350 to 470	300 (9.90)
Euglenophyceae	215 to 540	280 (9.24)
Phytoplankton		**2550 (84.19)**
Protozoans	17 to 95	58 (1.91)
Rotifers	100 to 270	182 (6.00)
Cladocerans	32 to 131	64(2.11)
Copepods	26 to 255	117(3.86)
Ostracods	21 to 112	58 (1.91)
Zooplankton		**479 (15.81)**
Total Zooplankton		**3029**

Vyas and Kumar (1968) made a study on productivity and periodicity of phytoplankton of the Indrasagar tank, Udaipur in relation to physico-chemical characteristics. Green algae dominated the phytoplankton both as regards number of species and number of individuals. A definite phytoplankton periodicity has been observed. The green algae dominating in the rainy and winter seasons and the blue –green algae during the summer.

Hulyal and Kaliwal (2009) studied dynamics of phytoplankton in relation to physico-chemical factors in Almatti reservoir of Bijapur district, Karnataka.

Tiwari and Chauhan (2006) observed maximum population of chlorophyceae in winter season. As compared to other classes of phytoplankton, the members of euglenoid were recorded least in number. The maximum population of euglenoids was recorded in winter.

Conclusion and Recommendations

Harni (Katgaon), which is one among the important reservoirs in Osmanabad district of Maharashtra, can contribute substantially to the fish production of the district, if developed on scientific lines. The state fisheries department should take initiatives to develop this reservoir for fish production. Attempts for scientific stocking of fast growing species, multiple harvesting, organizing marketing channels etc. are the immediate needs for sustainable utilization of fisheries of the reservoir. This would ensure more employment opportunities to the local masses.

The purchasing power of the fishermen would reflect directly on the magnitude of fishing operations. Therefore the government should come forward to provide subsidies to the fishermen for purchasing gears and crafts.

While evaluating the physico-chemical and biological properties of water, the following effective measures should be taken into consideration for management and conservation of reservoir fisheries.

1. Reservoir should be clear from submerged obstruction of tree trunks during summer season when the water level goes down and shore areas are exposed.

2. An effective stocking operation is possible only when the fingerlings are reared near the reservoir site by establishing a fish farm.
3. An effective stocking operation is possible only when the fingerlings are reared near the reservoir site by establishing a fish farm.
4. Stocking of fast growing commercially important species of fish particularly *Catla catla, Labeo rohita* and *Cirrhinus mrigal* should be maintained in the reservoir to procure a maximum sustained yield.
5. An effective control of predatory fishes should be needed for growth of commercially important fishes. Operation of specific gears to catch catfishes may be encouraged so as to facilitate development of Indian Major Carp fisheries. The society should offer more incentives to its members for catching more and more large catfishes and minnows from the reservoir.
6. The length of fingerlings stocked in the reservoir should be maintained above 15 cm to avoid large scale mortality.
7. A fisherman population should be settled around the reservoir and they may be trained in gill-net operation for fishing under deep water.
8. A committee comprising active members of the society should be constituted for ensuring the stocking of the reservoir with adequate number of advanced sized fingerlings of desried fish species in a definite ratio, as already recommended.
9. For the purpose of procuring a sustained yield of fish from the reservoir, various rules and regulations under the Indian Fisheries Act should be enforced wherever required.
10. Fishing should be effectively closed during monsoon (July to September) so that fishes will not be hampered to breed.

11. For the establishment and to have good recruitment rate, the spawners of Indian Major Carps and other quality exotic species like common carp and Grass carp should be stocked in the reservoir.
12. Emphasis should be given to periodical assessment of physico-chemical analysis of water and plankton community study.
13. The State Fisheries Department may also depute adequate technical as well as supervisory so as to guide the society for formulating, implementing and monitoring of the development programmes and also to check poaching and violation of fishery rules and regulations.

References

Ahirrao, S.D. and Mane, A.S. 2000. The Diversity of Ichthyofauna, Taxonomy and Fisheries from some Freshwaters of Parbhani District (M.S.). *J. Aqua. Biol.* 15 (1 & 2): 40-43.

Adwant, M.P. 1989. Limnological Studies on Godawari Basin at Nanded, Maharashtra, India. Ph.D. Thesis, Martahwada University, Aurangabad.

Agrawal, A.K. and Rajwar, G.S. 2010. Physico-chemical and Microbiological Study of Tehri Dam Reservoir, Garhwal Himalaya, India. *Journal of American Science*. 6 (6): 65-71.

Agarwal, S.S. 1978. Hydrobiological Survey of Janaktal Tank, Gwalior (Madhya Pradesh) India. Proceedings of All India Seminar on Icthyology. 20-26 pp.

Agarwal, S.S. 1980. Some Aspects of Limnology of Ramaua Dam with Special Reference to Phytoplankton and Zooplankton. Ph.D. Thesis, Jiwaji University, Gwalior.

Akbay, N., Anul, N., Yerti, S., Soyupak, S. and Yurteri, C. 1999. Seasonal Distribution of Large Phytoplankton in Keban Dam Reservoir. *Plank. Res.*, 21(4): 771-787.

Alikunhi, K.H. 1952. On the Food of Young Carp fry. J. Zool. Soc. India. 4: 77-84.

Annamalai, V. 1996. Return of Fishery Cooperatives in Martime States of India, Fish Technology Newsletter, Vol. III, Nos. 10 & 11, July-December, 1996, pp. 5-6.

Anderson, H.H. 1989. Notes on Indian Rotifers. *J. Asiatic Soc.* Bengal, Calcutta. 58: 345-358.

A.P.H.A. 1985. Standard Methods for the Examination of Water and Wastewater. 17th ed. American Public Health Association, Washington D.C.

Arora, H.C.1962. Studies on Indian rotifer. Part I. On a Small Collection of Illoricate Rotifer from Nagpur, India with Notes on their Bionomics. *J. Zool. Soc. India.* 14: 33-44.

Arora, H.C. 1963a. Studies on Indian Rotifer. Part II. Some Species of the Genus *Brachionus* from Nagpur. *J. Zool. Soc. India.* 15: 112-121.

Arora, H.C. 1964. Studies on Indian Rotifer. Part III. *J. Zool. Soc. India.* 16 (1-2): 1-6.

Arora, H.C. 1965. Studies on Indian Rotifer. Part VI. On a Collection of Rotifer from Nagpur, India with Four New Species and a New Variety. *Hydrobiologia.* 26: 444-456.

Arora, H.C. 1966. Responses of Rotifer to Variation in some Ecological Factors. Proc. Indian Acad. Sci. 63: 57-66.

Arora, H.C.1966a. Studies on Indian Rotifer. Part III. On *Brachionus calyciflorus* and some Varieties of the Species. *J. Zool. Soc. India.* 16: 1-6.

Ayoade, A.A., Agarwal, N.K. and Chandda Saklani, A. 2009. Changes in Physico-chemical Features and Plankton of Two Regulated High Altitude Rivers Garhwal Himalaya, India. European *Journal of Scientific Research.* 27(1): 77-92.

Baird, W.1850. The Natural History of the British Entomostracous. Roy. Soc. London; 1-364.

Banerjea, S.M. 1967. Water Quality and Soil Condition of Fish Ponds in some States of India in Relation to Fish Production. *Indian J.Fish.* 14(1&2): 115-144.

Battish, S.K. 1968. A Study of the Taxonomy and Seasonal Variation of Rotifers and Crustaceans. M.Sc. (Hons.) Thesis, Punjab University, Chandigarh, 199pp.

Battish, S.K. 1992. Freshwater Zooplankton of India. Oxford and IBH Publishing Co. Pvt. Ltd. New Delhi.

Battish, S.K. and Parminder Kumari.1986. Effect of Physico-chemical Factors on the Seasonal Abundance of Cladocera in Typical Pond at Village of Raqba, Ludhiana. Indian *Ecol.* 13 (1): 146-151.

Bays J S and T.L. Crisman.1983. Zooplankton and Trophic State Relationships in Florida Lakes. *Can. J. Fish. Aquat. Sci.* 40: 1813-1819.

Beaver, J.R. and Crisman, T.L. 1990. Use of Microzooplankton as an Early Indicator of Advancing Cultural Eutrophication. *Verh. Internat. Verein. Limnol.* 24: 532-537.

Bhowmik, M.L. 1968. Environmental Factors Affecting Fish Food in Freshwater Fisheries, Kalyani, West Bengal, India, Ph.D. Thesis, University of Kalyani, 238p.

Bhukaswan, T. 1977. Principles of Reservoir Fishery Management.

Boyd, C.E. and Tucker, C.S. 2009. Pond Aquaculture Water Quality Management. Springer International Edition, pp. 700.

Braj Mohan and Krishna Srinath. 2004. Role of Fisheries Cooperatives in Maharashtra. *Fishing chimes.* 23 (10 & 11): 90-92.

Canfield, T.J. and Jones, J.R. 1996. Zooplankton Abundance, Biomass, and Size Distribution in Selected Midwestern Waterbodies and Relation with trophic State, *J. Freshwat. Ecol.* 11: 171-181.

Chakrabarti, P.K. 1980. Studies on the Hydrobiology of some Freshwater Fisheries. Ph.D. Thesis, Burdwan University, 251p.

Chakravarthy, T.K. 1983. Role of Abiotic Factors in the Plankton Population of a Fish Pond at Maoghyr (Bihar). Proceedings of First Indian Symposium of Life Science. 171-175.

Chandanshive, N.E., Kamble, S.M. and Yadav, B.E. 2007. Fish Fauna of Pavana River of Pune, Maharashtra. *Zoos' Print Journal.* 22 (5): 2693-2694.

Chandrasekhar, S.V.A. 2006. Limnological Studies on Kondarkarla Lake Visakha District, Andhra Pradesh. In: Ecology of Lakes and Reservoirs (Ed.V.B. Sakhare), Daya Publishing House, Delhi, pp. 63-104.

Chakrapani, B.K., Krishna, M.B. and Srinivasa, T.S. 1996. A Report on the Water Quality, Plankton and Bird Populations of the Lakes in and around Bangalore and Maddur, Karnataka, India. Department of Ecology and Environment, Government of Karnataka. http://wgbis. ces. iisc. ernet. in/energy/water/paper/Tr-115/ref.htm.

Chakravarthy, N.M. and Asthaana, A.1989. Plankton Succession and Ecology of a Sewage Treated Pond in West Bengal. *Environment and Ecology*. 7: 549-554.

Charak, K.S. and Fayaz, F.A. 2006. Ecological Status of Salal Reservoir, Reasi, District Udhampur (J&K). *Fishing Chimes*. 26 (9): 38-40.

Chaudhary, C.S. 2008. Rajasthan: Fisheries Dept's Organizational Aspects and Status of Fisheries Development. *Fishing Chimes*. 28 (1): 158-159.

Chauhan, R. 1988. Seasonal Abundance of Zooplankton in Rewalsar Lake, H.P. *Geobios New Report*. 7(2): 117-121.

Chavan, R.J., Mohekar, A.D. and Hiware, C.J. 2006. Ecology and Behaviour of Zooplanktons in Manjara Project Reservoir in Maharashtra. In: Ecology of Lakes and Reservoirs (Dr. V.B. Sakhare, Ed.), Daya Publishing House, Delhi, pp. 151-162.

Chavan, S.P. 2006. An Evaluation of Fisheries Potential of Masoli Reservoir in Parbhani District of Maharashtra. In: Ecology of Lakes and Reservoirs (V.B. Sakhare, Ed.). pp. 186-189, Daya Publishing House, Delhi.

Choudhary, S. and Singh, D.K.1999. Zooplankton Populations of Boosra Lake at Muzaffarpur, Bihar. *Environment and Ecology*.17 (2): 444-448.

Chowdhary, S.K., Sharma, J.P. and Srivastava, J.B. 1978. On the Rotifer Fauna of Jammu Ponds. Proc. Indian Sci. Congr. (Abstracts).

Chrispin, C.L., Ananthan, P.S., Sugunan, V.V., Ramasubramanian, V., Pannikar, P., Landge, A.T. 2016. Fisheries and Management Status of Pechiparai Reservoir in Tamil Nadu. *Current World Environment,* 11(1): 233-242.

CIFRI. 1998. Ecological and Fisheries Status of Reservoirs in India- A Recent Survey. In: Das, Manas Kr. (ed.). *The Inland Fisheries News,* Newsletter of CICFRI. 3 (1): 1-2.

Das, P.K., Michael, R.G. and Gupta, A. 1996. Zooplankton Community in Lake Tasek a Tectonic Lake in Garo Hills, India. *Trop. Ecol.* 37(2): 257-263.

Das, R.K. 1996. Monitoring of Water Quality, its Importance in Disease Control. Paper Presented in Nat. Workshop on Fish and Prawn Disease, Epizootics and Quarantine Adoption in India. October 9, 1996. CICFRI. pp. 51-55.

Das, S.M. 1961. Hydrogen Ion Concentration, Plankton and Fish in Freshwater Eutrophic Lakes of India. *Nature.* 191 (478): 511-512.

Das, S.M. and Srivastava, V.K. 1956. Some New Observations on Plankton from Freshwater Ponds and Tanks of Lucknow, India. *Sci. and Cult.* 21: 446-467.

Datta, N.C., Bandyopadhyay, B.K., Das, M.K. and Bandyopadhyay, S.B. 1982. Diurnal Rhythm of some Physico-chemical Properties and Zooplankton in a Tropical Freshwater Pond in Calcutta, West Bengal. *Ind. J.Phy. Nat. Sc.* 2: 22-27.

David, A., Rao, N.G. and Ray, P. 1974. Tank Fishery Resources of Karnataka. Bull. Cent. Inland Fish. Res. Inst. Barrackpore. 20: p. 87.

Davie, T., 2002. Fundamentals of Hydrology. Routledge Publications.

Day, F.S. 1878. The Fishes of India,William and Sons Ltd., London.

De Beauchamp, P.M.1928. cou d' oeil sur less recherché recentes relative aux rotifers et less mthodes qui leur sont applicable.Bull.Biol.France et de la Belgique. 62: 51-125.

De Beauchamp, P.M. 1932. Contribution a l'etude du genre Ascomorpha et des processus digestifs chez les rotifers.*Bull.Soc.Zool.France.* 57: 428-449.

Desai, S.S., 1980. Fisheries of Nathsagar Reservoir. *India Today & Tomorrow.* 8(4): 181-161.

Deshmukh, U.S. 2001. Ecological Studies of Chhatri Lake, Amravati; with Special Reference to Planktons and Productivity, Ph.D. Thesis, Amaravati University, Amravati, pp. 175.

Devi, Sarla, B. 1997. Present Status, Potentialities, Management and Economics of Fisheries of Two Minor Reservoirs of Hyderabad. Ph.D. Thesis, Osmania University, Hyderabad.

Dewan, S.1973. Investigations into the Ecology of Fishes of a Mymensing Lake. Ph.D. Thesis, Bangladesh Agricultural University, Mymensingh, Bangladesh.

Dhanapathi, M.V.S.S.S. 1973. On the Occurrence of the Rare Rotifer Rotaria neptunia (Ehrenberg) in India. *Curr. Sci.* 42: 770.

Dhanapathi, M.V.S.S.S. 1974. A New Brachionid Rotifer Platyias quadricornis and hraensis subsp. Nov. from India. Curr. Sci. 43: 358. I. *Hydrobiologia.* 45: 357-372.

Dhanapathi, M.V.S.S.S. 1975b. Rotifers from Andhra Pradesh, India. *J.Linn.Soc. (Zool.),* 57: 85-94.

Dhanapathi, M.V.S.S.S. 1976a. Rotifers from Andhra Pradesh, India, III. Family Lecanidae including Two New Species. *Hydrobiologia.* 48: 9-16.

Dhanapathi, M.V.S.S.S 2000. Taxonomic Notes on the Rotifers from India (from 1889-2000). Pub. Indian Association of Aquatic Biologists, Hyderabad, pp. 178.

Dhavale, S.D., Lakde, H.M. and Lohare, S.D. 2009. Studies on Algal Flora and Physic-chemical Characteristics of Shikara Reservoir in Nanded District, Maharashtra. *Ecology and Fisheries.* 2 (2): 69-72.

Dixitulu, J.V.H. 1999. Render Indian Reservoirs Sustainably Fishful. *Fishing chimes*. 19 (2): 5-7.

Dubey, G.P. 2008. 50 Years of Fisheries of Development in Gandhi Sagar. *Fishing Chimes*. 28 (2): 8-16.

Edmondson, W.T. 1959. Rotifera, pp. 420-494. In: Freshwater Biology (eds. H.B. Ward and G. C. Whipple). (2nd Edition, W.T. Edmondson ed.) John Wiley & Sons. Inc. New York, 1248 pp.

Ellenberg, H. 1988. Bioindicator and Bioindication. Angewandte Okologie, Vol. 1, Stuttgart: Fisher, 226-262.

Elliott, J.A., Irish, A.E. and Reynolds, C.S. 2002. Predicting the Spatial Dominance of Phytoplankton in Light Limited and Incompletely mixed Eutrophic Water Column using the PROTECH model. *Fresh. Bio.* 47: 433-440.

EPA.1990. Biological Criteria: National Program Guidelines for Surface Waters. EPA-440/5-90- 004, Off. Water, Washington, DC.

Flossner, D.1972. Krebstiere, crustacea.kiemen-und Blattfusser Branchipooda, Fishlause, Branchiura.Die Teirwelt Deutschlands. 60: 501 pp.

Fokmare, A.K., Musaddiq, M. 2002. A Study of Physico-chemical Characteristics of Kapsi Lake and Purna River Waters in Akola District of Maharastra (India). *Nat. Environ. Poll. Tech.* 1: 261-263.

Fuller, D.R., Stemberger, R.S. and Gannon, J.E. 1977. Limnetic Rotifers as Indicators of Trophic change. *J. Elisha Mitchell. Sci. Soc.* 93: 104-113.

Gannon J.E. and R.S. Stemberger.1978. Zooplankton (Especially Crustaceans and Rotifers) as Indicators of Water Quality, Trans. Am. Micros. Soc. 97: 16-35.

Garg, R.K., Saksena, D.N., Rao, R.J. 2006b. Assessment of Physico-chemical Water Quality of Harsi Reservoir, District Gwalior, Madhya Pradesh. *J. Ecophysiol. Occupat. Health.* 6: 33-40.

Garg, R.K., Rao, R.J., Uchchariya, D., Shukla, G. and Saksena, D.N. 2010. Seasonal Variations in Water Quality and Major Threats to Ramsagar Reservoir, India. *African Journal of Environmental Science and Technology.* 4(2): 61-76.

Goel, P.K., Kulkarni, A.Y. and Khatavkar, S.D. 1968. Species Diversity in Phytoplankton Communities in a Few Freshwater Bodies in Southern Maharashtra. *Geobios.*15: 150-156.

Goel, P.K., Khatavkar, S.D., Kulkarni, A.Y. and Trivedy, R.K. 1986. Studies on Freshwater in Southwestern Maharashtra with Special Reference to their Chemistry and Phytoplankton. *Poll. Res.* 5(2): 79-84.

Goutam, Ranjan, Singh, N.P. and Singh, R.B. 2007. Physico-chemical Characteristics of Ghariyarwa Pond of Birganj, Nepal in Relation to Growth of Phytoplankton. *Nature Environment and Pollution Technology.* 6(4): 629-632.

Govind, B.V. 1963. Preliminary Studies on Plankton of the Tungabhadra Reservoir. *Indian J.Fish.*10 (1): 148-158.

Harilal, C.C. 2005. Phytoplankton Diversity of Two Rivers of Kerala with Special Reference to Aquatic Nutrients. *Poll. Res.* 24 (4): 773-776.

Harney, N.V., Sitre, S.R., N.S.Wadhave, N.S. and Nasare, P.N. 2008. Zooplankton Diversity in a Anthropologically Affected Freshwater Lake of Bhadrawati Town in Chandrapur District of Maharashtra. *Ecology and Fisheries.* 1 (1): 27-34.

Harshey, D.K., Shrivastav, A.K. and Patil, S.G. 1987. Studies on the Ecology of Freshwater Ostracoda. Part II. Population Ecology in Balsagar Tank, Jabalpur, M.P., India. *J.Curr.Biosci.* 4 (4): 127-134.

Hellawell J.M. 1986. Biological Indicators of Freshwater Pollution and Environmental Management. In Pollution Monitoring Series. Elsevier Applied Science Publishers, London, UK (p 546).

Henry, M. 1822. A Monograph of the Freshwater Entomostraca of New South Wales. Proc. Linn. Soc. New South Wales. 47: 26-52.

Hiware, C.J. 2006. Ichthoyfauna from Four Districts of Marathwada Region, Maharashtra, India. *Zoos' Print Journal*. 21 (1): 2137-2139.

Hosmani, S.P. and Bharthi, S.G. 1980. Limnological Studies in Ponds and Lakes of Dharwar. Comparative Phytoplankton Ecology of Four Water Bodies. *Phycos*. 19 (1): 27-43.

Hujare, M.S. 2005. Hydrobiological Studies on some Water Reservoirs of Hatkanangale Tahsil (Maharashtra). Ph.D. Thesis, Shivaji University, Kolhapur.

Hulyal, S.B. and Kaliwal, B.B. 2009. Dynamics of Phytoplankton in Relation to Physic-chemical Factors of Almatti Reservoir of Bijapur District, Karnataka State. *Environmental Monitoring and Assessment*. 153 (1-4): 45-59.

Hussain, M. 1977. Ecobiology of Freshwater Protozoa, Ph.D. Thesis, Osmania University, Hyderabad.

Hutchinson, G.E. 1957. A Treatise on Limnology. Introduction to Lake Biology and the Limnoplankton. John Wiley and Sons, New York, London, pp. 115.

Jennings, H.S. 1903. Rotatoria of the United States, II. A Monograph of the Rattulidae. *Bull. U.S. Fish Comm*. (1902): 273-352.

Jhingran Arun, G. and Sugunan,V.V. 1990. General Guidelines and Planning Criteria for Small Reservoir Fisheries Management. p.18. In: Jhingran Arun G. and V.K. Unnithan (eds). Reservoir Fisheries in India. Proc. of the Nat. Workshop on Reservoir Fisheries, 3-4 January 1990. Special Publication 3, Asian Fisheries Society, Indian Branch, Mangalore, India.

Jhingran, V.G. 1983. Fish and Fisheries of India. Hindustan Publishing Corporation, New Delhi.

Joshi, P.K. 2006. Physico-chemical Analysis of Water from Ekruk Reservoir (Maharashtra) for Potability. In: Ecology of Lakes and Reservoirs (V.B. Sakhare, Ed.) pp. 132-137, Daya Publishing House, Delhi.

Kadam, S.U., Gaikwad, J.M. and Babar, Md. 2006. Water Quality and Ecological Studies of Masoli Reservoir in Parbhani District, Maharashtra. In: Ecology of Lakes and Reservoirs (V.B. Sakhare, Ed.), pp. 163-175, Daya Publishing House, Delhi.

Kamath, G.S. 1980. The Fisheries Cooperatives in India-Performance, Problems and Prospects, Seminar on Fisheries Extension, Cochin, 8-10, December 1980.

Kant, S. and Raina, A.K. 1985. Limnological Studies of Two Ponds in Jammu. 1. Qualitative and Quantitative Distribution of Phytoplankton. *Zoologica Orientalis*. 2: 89-92.

Karr, J.R. 1991. Biological Integrity: A Long Neglected Aspect of Water Resource Management. *Ecological Applications*. 1: 66-84.

Kaushik, S. and Sharma, N. 1994. Physico-chemical Characteristics and Zooplankton Population of a Perennial Tank, Matsya Sarowar, Gwalior. *Environment and Ecology*. 12 (2): 429-434.

Keilhack, L.1909. Phyllopoda, In: A Brauers. Die Susswasserfauna Dautschlands. Jena; 10: 1-112.

Khabade, S.A. and Mule, M.B. 2010. Studies on Aquatic Insects in Relation to Physic-chemical Parameters of Anjani Reservoir in Sangli District of Maharashtra. In: Advances in Aquatic Ecology (Volume 3), Edited by V.B. Sakhare, pp. 141-147., Daya Publishing House, Delhi.

Khare, P.K. 1999. Phytoplankton as Indicators of Water Quality and Pollution Status of Jagat Sagar Pond, Chattarpur (M.P.). *Geobios New Reports*. 18(2): 107-110.

Khatri, T.C. 1985. A Note on the Limnological Characters of the Idukki Reservoir. *Indian J.Fish*. 32 (2): 267-269.

Kiran, B.R., Puttaiah, E.T. and Kamath, Devidas. 2007. Diversity and Seasonal Fluctuation of Zooplankton in Fish Pond of Bhadra Fish Farm, Karnataka. *Zoos' Print Journal.* 22(2): 2935-2936.

Kiran, B.R. and Puttaiah, E.T. 2010. Water Quality Assessment of Bhadra Reservoir of Karnataka with Reference to Physic-chemical Characteristics. In: Aquatic Ecosystem and its Management (Eds. K. Vijaykumar and B. Vasanthkumar), pp. 71-101, Daya Publishing House, Delhi.

Kodarkar, M.S., D.D. Diwan, N. Murugan, K.M. Kulkarni and Anuradha Ramesh. 1998. Methodology for Water Analysis (Physico-chemical, Biological and Microbiological). Indian Asso. of Aqua. Biologists, Hyderabad. pp. 12-102.

Korovchinsky, N.M. 1996. How many Species of Cladocera are there? *Hydrobiologia. 321:* 191-204.

Kumar, Arvind. 1995. Periodicity and Abundance of Plankton in Relation to Physic-chemical Characteristics of a Tropical Wetland of South Bihar. *Eco.Env. and Cons.* 1(1-4): 47-51.

Kumar, Arvind and Verma, P.K. 2002. Ecological Status of Masanjore Reservoir in Relation to Fisheries Management, Santal Pargana (Jharkhand), India. In: Ecology and Conservation of Lakes, Reservoirs and Rivers (Vol. 2), Edited by Arvind Kumar, ABD Pub. Jaipur.

Kumbhar, A.K., Kulkarni, D.A., Salunke, P.S. and Ghorpade, B.N. 2009. Study of Physical Parameters of Ujani Reservoir in Solapur District, Maharashtra. *Ecology and Fisheries.* 2(1): 69-72.

Lalrisanga, P.L., Landge, Asha and Prasad Umashankar. 2006. Stocking as a Tool for Inland Fisheries Management (Principles and Strategies). *Fishing Chimes.* 26 (2): 25-29.

Lokhande, M.V., Rathod, D.S., Shembekar, V.S. and Karadkhele, S.V. 2009. Seasonal Variation in Turbidity, Total Solids, Total Dissolved Solids, Total Suspended Solids of Dhanegaon Reservoir in Maharashtra. *Ecology and Fisheries.* 2 (1): 73-78.

Mahapatra, B.K., Vinod, K. and Mandal, B.K. 2004a. Studies on Chocolate Mahseer, *Neolissocheilus hexagonolepis* (McClelland) Fishery and the Cause of its Decline in Umiam Reservoir, Meghalaya. *J. Natcon.*16 (1): 199-205.

Mahapatra, D.K. 2003. Present Status of Fisheries of Hirakud Reservoir, Orissa. *Fishing Chimes.* 22 (10 & 11): 76-79.

Mali, R.P., Kamble, A.T. and Mudkhede, L.M. 2006. Physico-chemical Analysis of Bhategaon Reservoir in Parbhani District, Maharashtra. In: Ecology of Lakes and Reservoirs (V.B. Sakhare, Ed.) Pp. 176-180, Daya Publishing House, Delhi.

Mandal, B.K. 1972. Limnological Investigation on Freshwater Fisheries of Burdwan. Ph.D. Thesis, Burdwan University, West Bengal, India.

Manuilova, E.F. 1964. Cladocera of the Fauna of the USSR. Zool.Inst.Acad. Naukssar; 88: 1-327.

Maruthanayagam, C., Sasikumar, M. and Senthilkumar, C. 2003. Studies on Zooplankton Population in Thirukkulam Pond during Summer and Rainy Seasons. *Nature Environ. Pollut. Technol.* 2: 13-19.

Mathew, P.M. 1985. Seasonal Trends in the Fluctuations of Plankton and Physic-chemical Factors in a Tropical Lake (Govindgarh Lake, M.P.) and their Interrelationship. *J. Inland Fish.Soc. India.*17 (1&2): 11-24.

Melack, I.M. 1979. Photosynthetic Rates in Four Tropical Freshwaters. *Freshwater Biology.* 9: 555-571.

Michael, D.S. 1969. The Ecology of Vascular Hydrophytes in Lake Kasiba. *Hydrobiol.* 34: 448-464.

Michael, R, G. 1973. A Guide to the Study of Freshwater Organisms, *Madurai Univ. J. Suppl.*(Ed.) 1: 186 pp.

Michael, R.G. and Sharma, B.K. 1988. Fauna of India, Indian Cladocera (Crustacea: Branchiopda: Cladocera), Zoological Survey of India, Calcutta.

Michael, R.G. 1969. Seasonal Trends in Physico-chemical Factors and Plankton of Freshwater Fishponds and their Role in Fish Culture. *Hydrobiol.* 33(1): 145-160.

Mishra, S.R. 2005. Zooplankton and their Seasonal Variations in a Sewage Collecting River at Gwalior, Madya Pradesh. In: Advances in Limnology (Ed. S.R. Mishra), Daya Publishing House, Delhi, pp. 1-44.

Mohan, Braj. 2002. Economic Status of the Fishermen of Malamuzha Reservoir. In: Riverine and Reservoir Fisheries of India (Boopendranath, M.R., Meenakumari, B., Joseph, J., Sankar, T.V., Pravin, P. and Edwin, L. Eds.) P. 421-425, Society of Fisheries Technologists (India), Cochin.

Mohite, J.S. 2006. Ichthoyfauna of Reservoirs from Solapur District, Maharashtra. In: Ecology of Lakes and Reservoir (V.B. Sakhare, Ed.), pp. 181-185, Daya Publishing House, Delhi.

Moitra, S.K. and Bhattacharya, B.K. 1965. Some Hydrobiological Factors Affecting Plankton Production in a Fish Pond at Kalyani, West Bengal. *Ichthyologica.* 4(1-2): 8-12.

Mukherjee, Madhumita and Praharaj, Aloknath. 2009. Kangsabati Reservoir Fisheries Development: New Policy Approaches through Multidisciplinary Field Demonstrations to Rural People. *Fishing Chimes.* 29 (1): 112-121.

Mukherji, Manika and Nandi, N.C. 2006. Ecology, Biodiversity and Management of Rabindar Sarovar in Kolkata, West Bengal. In: Ecology of Lakes and Reservoirs (Dr. V.B.Sakhare), Daya Publishing House, Delhi,pp. 36-53.

Murugan, N., Murugavel, P. and Kodarkar, M.S. 1998. Cladocera (The Biology, Classification, Identification and Ecology), Publication No. 5, Indian Association of Aquatic Biologists, Hyderabad.

Myers, F.J. 1931. The Distribution of Rotifera on Mount Desert Island. *Amer. Mus. Novit.* 494: 1-12.

Myers, F.J. 1933. A New Genus of Rotifers (Dorria). *Jour. Roy. Micros. Soc.* 53: 118-121.

Myers, F.J. 1941. Lecane curvicornis var.miamiensis, New Variety of Rotatora, with Observations on the Feeding Habits of Rotifers. Notul. Nat. 75: 1-8.

Nagma, M. and Khan, M.A. 2015. Observations on Ichthyofauna and Water Quality of Pili Reservoir in District Bijnor of Uttar Pradesh. *International Journal of Fisheries and Aquatic Studies,* 2(6): 106-112.

Namboothiri, N.N. 2008. Present Status and Prospects of Fisheries Development in Malampuzha Reservoir-Palakkad, Kerala. *Fishing Chimes.* 28 (8): 10-13.

Nandan, S.N. and Ansari Ziya. 1999. Ecological Study of Algae from Mausam River Flowing through Malegaon City (Maharashtra). BRI'S *JAST.* 11 (1): 31-38.

Nandan, S.N. and Jain, D.S. 2005. Study of Algae Tolering Organic Pollution of Sonvad Dam and Devbhane Dam of Maharashtra. In: Advances in Limnology (Ed. S.R. Mishra, Daya Publishing House, Delhi, pp. 214-222.

Nandan, S.N. and Mahajan, S.R. 2006. Studies on Algae of Polluted Lakes of Jalgaon (Maharashtra): Role of Blue Green Algae. In: Ecology of Lakes and Reservoirs (Dr. V.B. Sakhare), pp. 54-62.

Nandan, S.N. and Patel, R.J. 1985a. Seasonal Variations of Phytoplankton in the Vishwamitri River, Baroda. In: Advances in Applied Phycology (Eds. A.C. Shukla and S.N. Pandey), pp. 262-269.

Nandan, S.N. and Patel, R.J. 1986. Assessment of Water Quality of Vishwamitri River by Algal Analysis. India. *J.Environ. Hlth.* 29 (2): 160-161.

Nasare, P.N., Wadhave, N.S., Harney, N.V. and Sitre, S.R. 2009. Studies on Phytoplankton Diversity of Vinjasan Lake in Bhadrawati Town of Chandrapur District, Maharashtra. *Ecology and Fisheries.* 2 (1): 95-100.

Nayar, C.K.G. 1964. Morphometric Studies on the Rotifer *Brachionus calyciflorus* Pallas. *Curr. Sci.* 33: 469-470.

Nayar, C.K.G. 1965a. Cyclomorphosis of *Brachionus calyciflorus* Pallas. *Hydrobiologia*. 25: 538-544.

Nayar, C.K.G. 1965b. Taxonomic Notes on the Indian Species of Keratella (Rotifera). *Hydrobiologia*. 26: 457-462.

Nees, J. 1946. Development and Status of Pond Fertilization in Central Europe. *Trans. Amer.Fish.Soc.*, 76: 355-358.

Niture, S.D. and Chavan, S.P. 2009. Crafts and Gears used in Yeldari Reservoir, Maharashtra. *Ecology and Fisheries*. 2 (1): 113-120.

Pace M J. 1986.An Empirical Analysis of Zooplankton Community Size Structure Across Lake Trophic Gradients, *Limnol. Oceanogr*. 31: 45-55.

Pandey, J. and Verma, A. 2004. The Influence of Catchment on Chemical and Biological Characteristics of Two Freshwater Tropical Lakes of Southern Rajasthan. *J.Environ.Biol*. 25: 81-87.

Pandit, S.V., Vaidya, V.V. and Joshi, P.P. 2007. Studies on Zooplankton Diversity of Pravara River, near Sangamner Dist. Ahmednagar, M.S. *J.Aqua.Biol*. 22 (1): 33-38.

Pathak, S.C. 1990. Harnessing Reservoirs for Increasing Fish Production. p 9-12. In: Jhingran Arun G. and V.K. Unnithan (eds). Reservoir Fisheries in India. Proc. of Nat. Workshop on Reservoir Fisheries, 3-4 January 1990. Spl. Publ. 3. Asian Fisheries Society, Indian Branch, Mangalore, India.

Pathak, S.K. and Mudgal, L.K. 2005. Limnology and Biodiversity of Fish Fauna in Virla Reservoir, M.P. India. *Environment Conservation Journal*, 6(1): 41-45.

Patil, C.S. and Gouder, B.Y.M. 1985. Ecological Study of Freshwater Zooplankton of a Subtropical Pond (Karnataka, India). *Int. Revue Ges. Hydrobiol*. 70: 279-287.

Patil, C.S. and Gouder, B.Y.M. 1989. Freshwater Invertebrates of Dharwad, Prasaranga, Karnatak University, Dharwad.

Patil, P.V. and Kulkarni, A.N. 2010. Diurnal Changes of some Physico-chemical Factors in Thodga Reservoir of Latur District in Maharashtra. In: Advances in Aquatic Ecology (Vol. 3), Ed. V.B. Sakhare, pp. 158-162., Daya Publishing House, Delhi.

Pawar, S.K., Madlapure, V.R. and Pulle, J.S. 2003. Study of Zooplanktonic Community of Sirur Dam Water near Mukhed in Nanded District (M.S.), India.*J.Aqua.Biol.*18 (2): 37-40.

Pearsall, W.H. 1921. A Theory of Diatoms Periodicity. *J.Ecol.* 1 (2): 165-183.

Peerapornpisal, Y., Sonthichai, W., Somdee, T., Mulsin, P. and Rott, E. 1999. Water Quality and Phytoplankton in the Mae Kuang Udomtara Reservoir, Chiang Mai, Thailand. *J. Sci. Fac. Cmu.* 26(1): 25-43.

Pennak, R.W. 1978. Freshwater Invertebrates of the United States. 2nd Edition, John Willey Sons, New York, 803 pp.

Piska Ravi Shankar, Sarla Devi B., and Chary Divakara K. 2000. The Present Status of Ibrhimbagh, a Minor Reservoir of Hyderabad. *Fishing chimes.* 20 (2): 41-43.

Pradhan, Arunava, Bhaumik Pranami, Das Sumana and Mishra, Madhusmita. 2008. Phytoplankton Diversity as Indicator of Water Quality for Fish Cultivation. *Am. J. Environ. Sci.* 4 (4): 406-411.

Pradhan, Prasenjit, Sunirmal Giri and Susanta Kumar Chakraborty. 2006. Ecological Gradients Determining the Density and Diversity of Rotifer in a Freshwater River System of South West Bengal, India. *J. Aqua. Biol.* 21(1): 19-28.

Rajashekar, M., Vijaykumar, K. and Zebra Paerveen. 2010. Seasonal Variations of Zooplankton Community in Freshwater Reservoir of Gulbarga Distrct, Karnataka, South India. *International Journal of Systems Biology.* 2 (1): 6-11.

Raje, S.G. and Singh, V.V. 1993. Towards Prosperity: Maharashtra Fisheries March Through Cooperatives. *Fishing Chimes.* 13 (6): 51-53.

Ramesh M., Saravanan M., Pradeepa G. 2007. Studies on the Physico-chemical Characteristics of the Singallunar Lake, Coimbatore, South India. In Proceeding National Seminar on Limnol. Maharana Pratap University of Agric. Technology, Udaipur, India.

Ranjan, Goutam, Singh, N.P. and Singh, R.B. 2007. Physico-chemical Characteristics of Ghariyarwa Pond of Birganj, Nepal in Relation to Growth of Phytoplankton. *Nature Environment and Pollution Technology*. 6 (4): 629-632.

Rathore, L.K., Sharma, B.K. and Dangi, P.L. 2017. Fish Biodiversity and Fisheries Potential of Reservoir Udaisagar (Udapur), Rajasthan). *International Journal of Fisheries and Aquatic Studies*, 5(3): 587-592.

Rawat, M.S. and Sharma, R.C. 2010. Analysis of Zooplankton Population in Garhwal Himalayan Lake, Deoria Tal, Uttarakhand. In: Aquatic Ecosystem and its Management (Eds. K. Vijaykumar and B. Vasanthkumar), Daya Publishing House, Delhi, pp. 102-109.

Reddy, B.S. and Parameshwar, K.S. 2015. Ichthyofaunal Diversity of Chandrasagar and Ramanpad Reservoirs in Mahabubnagar District, Telngana. International Journal of Fisheries and Aquatic Studies, 3(2): 40-49.

Renuga, K. and Ramnibai, R. 2006. Contribution to the Distribution of Freshwater Copepods of Kanchipuram District of Tamil Nadu. In: Ecology of Lakes and Reservoirs (Dr. V.B. Sakhare), Daya Publishing House, Delhi, pp. 143-150.

Renuga, K. and Ramnibai, R.2010. Zooplankton Composition Present in Krishnagiri Reservoir, Tamil Nadu, India. *Current Biotica*. 3 (4): 519-522.

Rao, K.D.S., Ramakrishniah, M., Karthikeyan, M., Sukumaran, P.K .2003. Limnology and Fish yield Enhancement through Stocking in Markonahalli Reservoir (Cauvery River System). *J. Inland Fish. Soc.India*. 35: 20-27.

Rao, M. and Ram Gopal. 2008. Andhra Pradesh: Fisheries Dept's Organizational Aspects and Status of Fisheries Development. *Fishing Chimes*. 28 (1): 152-154.

Ravinder, B., Narasimha, R.K. and Benarjee, K.G. 2016. Physico-chemical Parameters and Ichthyofauna Abundance of Dharmasagar Reservoir of Warangal District (T.S.), India. *International Journal of Fisheries and Aquatic Studies*, 4(2): 106-108.

Rawat M.S. and Sharma R.C. 2005. Phytoplankton Population of Garhwal Himalayam Lake Deoria Tal, Uttranchal. *J. Ecophysiol. Occupat.Health*. 5: 73-76.

Rawat, M.S., Sharma R.C. 2010. Analysis of Zooplankton Population in Garhwal Himalayan Lake, Deoria Tal, Uttarakhand. In: Aquatic Ecosystem and its Management (Ed. K.Vijaykumar and B. Vasanthkumar), Daya Publishing House, Delhi, pp. 102-109.

Reid, G.K. 1961. Ecology of Inland Waters and Estuaries, Reinhold Publishing Corporation, New York, 375 p.

Sahai, R. and Sinha, A.B.1969. Investigation on Bioecology of Inland Waters of Gorakhpur (U.P., India) Limnology of Ramgarh Lake. *Hydrobiol*. 34 (3&4): 433-477.

Sahib, S.S. 2004. Physico-chemical and Zooplankton of the Schendurni River, Kerala. *J.Ecobiol*. 16: 159-160.

Saikia, S.K. and Das, D.N. 2003. Diversity Indices of Zooplankton and Water Quality in Two Freshwater Ponds of Arunachal Pradesh, India. *Geobios*. 30 (2-3): 113-116.

Sakhare, V.B. 1999. Fisheries of Yeldari Reservoir, Maharashtra. *Fishing Chimes*. 19 (8): 45-47.

Sakhare,V.B. 2001. Ichthyofauna of Jawalgaon Reservoir in Solapur District of Maharashtra. *J.Aqua.Biol*.16 (1&2): 31-33.

Sakhare,V.B. 2005. Water Quality of Hingni (Pangaon) Reservoir and its Significance to Fisheries. Advances in Limnology (ed. S.R. Mishra, Dhar), Daya Publishing House, New Delhi, pp. 231-235.

Sakhare,V.B. 2006. Ecology of Jawalgaon Reservoir in Solapur District, Maharashtra. In: Ecology of Lakes and Reservoirs (V.B. Sakhare, Ed.), pp. 16-35, Daya Publishing House, Delhi.

Sakhare, V.B. 2007. Reservoir Fisheries and Limnology, Narendra Publishing House, Delhi, pp 187.

Sakhare, V.B. 2007. Wan Reservoir (Beed District; Maharashtra): Ecology and Fisheries. *Fishing Chimes*. 27 (6): 23-26.

Sakhare, V.B. 2009. Impact of Tilapia on Indigenous Fishes: A Case Study of Ramdara Reservoir in Osmanabad district of Maharashtra. Final Report of Minor Research Project, University Grants Commission, Western Regional Offcie, Pune, pp. 28.

Sakhare, V.B. and Jetithor, S.G. 2009. Ichthyofauna of Reservoirs from Osmanabad District, Maharashtra. In: Aquatic Biology and Aquaculture (V.B. Sakhare, Ed.), Pp 164-170, Manglam Publication, Delhi.

Sakhare, V.B. and Joshi, P.K. 2002. Ecology of Palas-Nilegaon Reservoir in Osmanabad District, Maharashtra. *J.Aqua.Biol.* 18 (2): 17-22.

Sakhare, V.B. and Joshi, P.K. 2003. Reservoir Fishery Potential of Parbhani District of Maharashtra. *Fishing Chimes*. 23 (5): 13-16.

Sakhare, V.B. and Joshi, P.K. 2004. Present Status of Reservoir Fisheries in Maharashtra. *Fishing Chimes*. 24 (8): 56-60.

Sakhare, V.B. and P.K. Joshi. 2006. Plankton Diversity in Yeldari Reservoir, Maharashtra. *Fishing Chimes*. Vol. 25 (12): 23-25.

Sankarasubbaiyan and V. Ramachandra Menon. 1984. Reservoir Fisheries in Tamilnadu, Present Status, Future Programmes and Policy Issues. p. 251-264. In: Srivastava K. and S. Vathsala (eds). Strategy for Development of Inland Fishery Resources In India. Key Issues in Production and Marketing. Proc. of Nat. Workshop on Dev. of Inland Fishery Resources, Nov. 1-3, 1983 at Ahemadabad.

Santhanam, R. and Krishnamurthy, K. 1985. On Planktonic Rotifers. 3rd All India Congr. Zool. (Abstracts).

Sharma, B.D. 2008. Fisheries Development in Himachal Pradesh: Present Status and Outlook. *Fishing Chimes*. 28 (1): 89-91.

Sharma, B.K. and Lyngdoh. 2003. Abundance and Ecology of Net and Phytoplankton of a Subtropical Reservoir of Meghalaya (N.E. India), Ecology, Environment and Conservation. 9 (4): 497-503.

Sharma, B.K. and Lyngsker Clarobian. 2003. Plankton Communities of a Subtropical Reservoir of Meghalaya (N.E. India). *Indian Journal of Animal Sciences*.73 (2): 209-215.

Sharma, B.K. 2009. Composition, Abundance and Ecology of Phytoplankton Communities of Loktak Lake, Manipur, India. *Journal of Threatened Taxa*. 1(8): 401-410.

Sharama, Shailendra, Wala, Hemendra and Sharma, Rekha. 2020. Ichthyofaunal Diversity and Productivity of Dilawara Reservoir of Dhar District, Madhya Pradesh. *International Journal of Fisheries and Aquatic Studies*, 8(5): 375-379.

Shastri, Yogesh. 2005. Physico-chemical Characteristics of a Small Percolation Tank. In: Advances in Limnology (Ed. S.R. Mishra), Daya Publishing House, Delhi, pp. 253-257.

Shastri,Yogesh and Bhogaonkar, P.Y. 2006. Water Quality of Talwade Reservoir of Nashik District, Maharashtra. In: Ecology of Lakes and Reservoirs (V.B. Sakhare, Ed.), pp. 138-142.

Sinha, K.K. and Sinha, D.K. 1993. Seasonal Trends in Physico-chemical Factors and Zooplankton in a Freshwater Pond of Munger, Bihar. *J.Ecobiol.* 5(4): 299-302.

Singh, Meena and Sinha, R.K. 1995. Diel Variation of Water Quality and Zooplankton Community in a Freshwater Pond of Patna, Bihar. *Eco.Env. and Cons.* 1(1-4): 57-64.

Singh, Y. 1979. Ecological Studies on River Algae with Special Reference to Bacillariophyceae. Ph.D. Thesis, Lucknow University, Lucknow.

Sisodiya Manish, Kunwar Chaudhary Lalit and Bhardhwaj, Seema. 2018. Fish Diversity in relation to Physico-chemical Characteristics of Haro Reservoir of Ghatol, Banswara (Rajasthan). *Internatioal Journal of Fisheries and Aquatic Studies*, 6(4): 199-202.

Sivakumar, K. and Karuppasamy, R. 2008. Factors Affecting Productivity of Phytoplankton in a Reservoir of Tamil Nadu, India. *American –Eurasian Journal of Botany*. 1 (3): 99-103.

Sprules, W.G. 1977. Crustacean Zooplankton Communities as Indicators of Limnological Conditions: An Approach using Principal Component Analysis. *J. Fish. Res. Board Can.* 34: 962-975.

Sreenivasan, A.1964. The Limnology, Primary Production, and Fish Production on a Tropical Pond. *Limnol. Oceanogr.* 9(4): 391-396.

Sreenivasan, A. 1976. Limnological Studies and Primary Production in Temple Pond Ecosystem. *Hydrobiol.* 48: 117-123.

Sreenivasan, A. 1991. Reservoir Fisheries of India- An Overview Report to the IRDC.

Sreenivasan, A. 1998. Intrgrated Development of Reservoir Fisheries of India: Production to Marketing. *Fishing Chimes*. 18 (1): 60-63.

Sreenivasan, A. 2000. Large Dams be Damned: They are not Eco-Friendly. *Fishing Chimes*. 20 (1): 81-83.

Srivastava, U.K., Desai, D.K., Gupta,V.K., Rao, S.S., Gupta, G.S., Raghavachari, M. and Vatsala, S. 1985. Inland Fish Marketing in India- Reservoir Fisheries,Vol. 4 (A&B). Concept Publishing Co; New Delhi, pp (A) 403 & (B) 1184.

Sugunan, V.V., 1990. Reservoir Fisheries Management. In: Sugunan V.V. and U. Bhowmick (eds) Technologies for Inland Fisheries Development. Central Inland Capture Fisheries Research Institute, Barrackpore, India, pp. 153-164.

Sugunan, V.V. 1995. Reservoir Fisheries of India. FAO Fisheries Tech. Report 345. Daya Publishing House, Delhi.

Sugunan, V.V. and Yadava, Y.S. 1991b. Feasibility Studies for Fisheries Development of Nongamahir Reservoir, CIFRI, Barrackpore, pp. 30.

Sundaramoorthy, K.D. 2008. Tamil Nadu: Fisheries Dept's Organizational Aspects and Status of Fisheries Development. *Fishing Chimes*. 28 (1): 155-157.

Sunkad, B.N. and Patil, H.S. 2004. Water Quality Assessment of Fort Lake of Belgaum (Karnataka) with Special Reference to Zooplankton. *J. Environ. Biol.* 25: 99-102.

Surve, P.R., Ambore, N.E., Pulle, J.S. 2005. Hydrobiological Studies of Kandhar Dam Water, District Nanded (M.S.), India. *J. Ecophysiol. Occupat. Health.* 5: 61-63.

Talwar, P.K. and Jhingran, A.G. 1991. Inland Fishes of India and Adjacent Countries. Vol. I & II. Oxford & IBH Publ. Co. Pvt. Ltd. New Delhi.

Tewari, D.D., Mishra, S.M. 2005. Limnological Study during Rainy Season of Seetadwar Lake at Shrawasti District. *J. Ecophysiol. Occupat.Health.* 5: 71-72.

Thirumathal, K. 2006. Cladocerans of Amaravathy Reservoir, Udumalpet, Coimbatore District, Tamil Nadu, India. In: Ecology of Lakes and Reservoirs (Dr. V.B. Sakhare), Daya Publishing House, Delhi, pp. 105-110.

Tideman, E.M. 2000. Watershed Management: Guidelines for Indian Conditions. Omega Scientific Publishers, New Delhi.

Tiwari, Ashesh and Chauhan, S.V.S. 2006. Seasonal Phytoplanktonic Diversity of Kitham Lake, Agra. *J.Environ.Biol.* 27 (1): 35-38.

Tripathi, S.D. 2007. Problems and Prospects of Fisheries Development in India. *Fishing Chimes*. 27 (1): 100-106.

Trivedy, R.K. and Goel, P.K. 1984. Chemical and Biological methods for Water Pollution Studies. Environmental Publications, Karad.

UNEP. 1996. World Resources 1996-1997, The Urban Environment United Nations Environmental Program. New York. USA.

Unni, K.S. 1985. Comparative Limnology of Several Reservoirs in Central India. *Int. Revue gesamten Hydrobiologia*, 70 (6): 845-856.

Uttangi, J.C. 2001. Conservation and Management Strategy for the Water Fowls of Minor Irrigation Tank Habits and their Importance as Stopover Site in Dharwad Dist. In: Hosetti, Venkatsehwarlu (Eds.).Trends in Wildlife and Management, Daya Publishing House, Delhi, pp. 179-221.

Valsangkar, S.V. 1980. Economic Rehabilitation of Fishermen in Yeldari Reservoir. *India Today and Tomorrow.* 8(4): 162-163.

Valsangkar, S.V. 1993. Mahseer Fisheries of Koyana River (Shivajisagar) in Maharashtra: Scrap to Bonanza. *Fishing Chimes.* 12 (10): 15-19.

Vass, K.K. and Sugunan, V.V. 2009. Status of Reservoir Fisheries in India. In: Status of Reservoir Fisheries in Five Asian Countries (Eds. Sena S. De Silva and Upali S. Amarsinghe), NACA Monograph No. 2, Network of Aquaculture Centers in Asia –Pacific, Bangkok, Thailand, pp. 31-54.

Vass, K.K., N.P. Shrivastava, P.K. Katiha and A.K. Das. 2009. Enhancing Fishery Productivity in Small Reservoir in India. A Technical Manual. World Fish Center Technical Manual No. 1949. The World Fish Center, Penang, Malaysia. 19 pp.

Venu,P. and Seshavatharam,V. 1984. Phytoplankkton Production in Relation to Physic-chemical Conditions in Lake Kondakarla. Proc. Indian Natn. Sci. Acad. B51 No. 6 pp. 588-595.

Verma, P.K. 2002. Limnological Investigation of Badua Reservoir with Reference to Fish Production and Conservation, Bhagalpur (Bihar State), India. In: Ecology and Conservation of Lakes, Reservoirs and Rivers (Vol. 2) (Ed. Arvind Kumar), ABD Pub. Jaipur, 105-135.

Verma, S.R. and Shukla, G.R. 1970. The Physico-chemical Conditions of Kamla Nehru Tank, Muzzafarnagar (U.P.) in Relation to the Biological Productivity. *Environment.* 12: 110-128.

Victor, R. and Fernando, C.H. 1979. The Freshwater Ostracods (Crustacea-Ostracoda) of India. Records of the Zoological Survey of India. 74: 147-242.

Vinod, K., Mahapatra, B.K. and Mandal, B.K. 2003b. Studies on the Growth of Stocked Indian Major Carps and their Impact on Fisheries in Umiam Reservoir, Meghalaya. *Aquacult.* 4 (2): 247-252.

Vinod, K., Mahapatra, B.K. and Mandal, B.K. 2007. Umiam Reservoir Fisheries of Meghalaya (Eastern Himalayas) Strategies for Optimization. *Fishing Chimes.* 26 (10): 8-15.

Vinod, K., Margaret, A.M.R., Mandal, B.K. and Murugkar, H.V. 2000. Aermonas Disease in Common Carp (*Cyprinus carpio*) of Umiam Reservoir, Meghalaya. *Environment and Ecology.* 18 (1): 100-103.

Vyas, L.N. and Kumar, H.D. 1968. Studies on the Phytoplankton and other Algae of Indrasagar Tank, Udaipur, India. *Hydrobiol.* 31 (3-4): 421-434.

Yousuf, A.R. and Parveen, M. 1990. Phytoplankton Dynamics in Dal Lake, Kashmir. In: Contributions to the Fisheries of Inland Open Water Systems in India (Ed. A.G. Jhingran, V.K. Unnithan and Amitabha Ghosh), Inland Fisheries Society of India, pp. 58-63.

Wagh, G.K. and Ghate, H.V. 2003. Freshwater Fish Fauna of the Rivers Mula and Mutha, Pune, Maharashtra. *Zoos' Print Journal.* 18 (1): 977-981.

Welch, P.S. 1948. Limnological Methods. Mc Graw-Hill Book Company, Inc., New York.

Wetzel, R.G. 1975. Limnology, Saunders Publishing, USA, 767pp.

Wetzel, R.G. 2001. Limnology: Lakes and River Ecosystems. 3rd Edition. Academic Press.

Whitton, B.A. and Patts, M. 2000. The Ecology of Cyanobacteria. Kluwer Academic Publishers, Netherlands.

Index

O

P

R

S

T

W

Z

❑ ❑ ❑ ❑ ❑